CAT SC

2020

Will
You
Die?

A NOVEL BY

D. KOTSCHWAR, M.D.

Published by Silversmith Press—Houston, Texas
www.silversmithpress.com

The views and opinions expressed here in belong to the author and do not necessarily represent those of the publisher.

ISBN 978-1-961093-36-2 (Softcover Book)
ISBN 978-1-961093-43-0 (Hardcover Book)
ISBN 978-1-961093-37-9 (eBook)

To those influenced.

ACKNOWLEDGEMENTS

To the balcony folk who cheered this author and gave their input: Liz, Sherry, Annaliesa, Sharon, Shirley, Carolyn, Christi, Phillip Max, Kay, and Shauna.

To the courageous folk who endured the writing of this novel: Tom, Phyllis, and Nancy.

To teachers of the art of writing—Jerry Jenkins, Joanna Hunt, and Mary Jo Gremling. I remain a student.

There are more things in Heaven and Earth,
Horatio, than are dreamt of in your philosophy.

—William Shakespeare, *Hamlet*, Act I, Scene V

1

"If you're pregnant, you'd better get rid of it!" Jethro jumped out of bed and pounded into the bathroom. "Before I get rid of you."

Tanya crouched beside the toilet. She dropped the home pregnancy strip onto the bathroom tiles.

"And that's no idle threat," thundered Jethro. His nose rings flared in the mirror above the sink. His arm muscles shivered beneath his tattoos.

Tanya raised her arms to shield her head, ignoring the divider that hid his naked lower body.

"I'll take care of it," she pleaded.

Jethro pulled on his jogging shorts, tucked his shirt into the waistband, and headed for the door.

"Just remember what I told you."

Tanya wedged deeper between the sink and the toilet. "I said I'll take care of it." She shuddered on the cold tiles, dust and hair hiding in the corner.

"I'll take care of it," she repeated.

The kitchen door slammed. Boots retreated down the stairs.

The door to the garage slapped open.

A car engine roared from the garage beneath the floor. The plywood walls shook. Dishes rattled in the cupboard.

Tires splattered the slush. Wheels squealed.

Then gravel spit.

The car roared to the end of the driveway.

Wheels screeched again. Tires whined down a paved road into the distance.

Silence.

Tanya waited.

Dust drifted downward in a shaft of early morning light. A cold draft skirted the floor. *The garage door must still be open.*

She twisted her ear to the floor and listened.

Quiet.

She lunged for the bed and wrestled the blankets to cover her naked chest. Her elbow wobbled as she craned her neck for a peek at the mirror above the dresser. The digital date clock back spelled 7:20 a.m.

It's already January 20th. Seems like the New Year's Eve party was just last week. This year—2020—was supposed to be the best.

She sniffed.

Another sniff.

She breathed.

A longer breath this time.

I missed my period in December. Missed it again in January. What a way to start the year.

Quiet.

Gurgling in the pipes above the ceiling. *The upstairs neighbor's morning ritual.* Fading.

Silence.

Her icy fingers found the phone beneath her pillow.

2

Maia bopped the phone on her side of the bed. *Time to get up.* She moaned. *Already.*

Jonathan jerked in the bed next to her. *Must be dreaming.* Her mind mapped his miseries. *An abusive home. Escaped to military service in a war zone. Now back. A civilian again.*

Jonathan snored. Maia surveyed the long, skinny bumps silhouetted in the early morning light. *Jonathan is not that good. Nobody is that good anymore. But he IS a nice guy.*

She studied the ceiling behind the mirror above the bed, water stains sneaking from corner to corner. *This is no way to live. This is no way to get the life I want.*

The mirror above the bed reflected bad bedhead. Even in the dimness, blue tips jutted above her auburn roots. *As soon as I get a paycheck, I need to get to the salon.* Maia furrowed her fingers through her hair.

Can't see my freckles, though.

She fisted the pillow.

This is a hard pillow.

Maia untangled her generous body from the blankets and slid her white legs onto the carpet below.

She tiptoed to his kitchen, sidestepping the head bunting of his cat.

Maia found a coffee mug in the cupboard. The cup steamed its contents before the gentle bump and drip. *This is no way to spend the life I've been given.*

A shaft of dawn light slid beneath the blinds. *Morning should be here soon.* She flatfooted to the plaid couch in the living room. She perched her mug between car magazines on the side table. "There must be peace somewhere," she muttered.

Jonathan rounded the corner, tousled blond hair covering his eyes. "Hello, stranger."

He batted his bangs, his eyes bleary. He corrected himself. "Well, you're no stranger to me. Not anymore, anyhow."

Maia chuckled. "Not anymore, anyhow."

Jonathan headed to the kitchen, cursing the cat hair that stuck to his feet. "No cat hair in the coffee, anyhow," he chuckled. "I told you I keep a clean place."

Maia took a sip. "Pretty private, anyhow."

"Yeah, works for me."

Maia finished the last of her coffee, her palms lingering on the warm mug, then placed it on the counter. "Looks like I need to leave for work."

"Yeah. Hope it's not too slippery out there."

Jonathan grabbed the mug and put it in the dishwasher. "Oh, be sure to remember the party I told you about last night. Should be at Desai's. Saturday night."

"I'll think about it. Depends on how busy work is."

"Well, think about it." He followed her to the door, opened it. "My band is booked for the next two nights, and the backup drummer is out of town."

He cleared his throat. "So maybe I'll see you there on Saturday?"

She bounded down the steps in the predawn darkness. "Nicely private," she muttered. "Works for me."

From the driveway, she glimpsed Jonathan still in his boxers, the front door open, the light still on behind him.

* * *

"Maia, can you pick me up?" Tanya urged. "Like, NOW?"

"I'm just leaving a friend's apartment on my way to work." Maia hesitated. "There are slick patches out here." She let go of the steering wheel. The jeep righted itself. She squinted. "They're hard to see."

"It has to be NOW. As soon as you can get here." Tanya's voice quivered. "Or never," she trailed.

Blazing pink. More drama.

Maia rerouted, watching the early morning shadows for hidden ice. *But Tanya sounded scared this time.*

She pumped her brakes for the red light, then texted her work, "Will be late."

The jeep lights narrowed to a potholed street. Maia spotted a light still on outside a dark apartment window. She stopped half a block away.

Tanya emerged from the shadows with three lumpy plastic bags. She waved into the headlights.

Tanya bounded in, shivering. "I might be pregnant," she explained, breathless. "Jethro is pissed. Told me to get rid of it. Like, yesterday."

Maia said nothing, backtracking to her rental house.

Tanya looked anxiously at Maia, then put on her cap. "I'll need a place to stay." She grabbed her gloves from the top bag and put them on.

Maia looked in the rearview mirror, her foot cautious on the accelerator.

Tanya tugged her gloves above her wrists. "A couch will do. Anywhere that's safe."

"I'm not sure I can guarantee that." Maia checked the rearview mirror again. "Do you still have your cell phone on you?"

"Sorry. Forgot about that."

"Well, you need to get rid of it. Fast." Maia checked the rearview mirror a third time.

"The pregnancy or the phone?"

"The phone." Maia swerved again. "Like, before I get home from work."

"I put the phone in airplane mode. Will that do it?" Tanya removed her gloves and placed her fingers near the warm air vent.

"You need to get rid of the blasted phone!" Maia hit the garage door opener and braked.

3

Two hours after she left Jonathan and deposited Tanya at her place, Maia was standing inside Fuchsia Salon. Her phone read 9:50 a.m.

"Bonjour," dripped a sassy voice behind a faux column. Maia stopped moving her numb toes and peeked at her tapered stilettos. *Clean.*

She turned.

A black pageboy haircut appeared, framing the porcelain face, crimson lipstick outlining the manicured lips. Perfect teeth, coiffed smile.

"I'm the new intern here," Maia stammered.

"Oh, the intern in business and economics," the saucy voice lamented. "From the university."

A feather-tipped pencil soon graced the perfect hands. "Well, stand over there. I need to see if you're presentable for us and not just for your professors. We have a discerning clientele, you know."

Maia took a shallow breath and walked to the full-length mirror. She blinked at the white knobby knees below her best leather skirt. She tilted her head to catch the light, shimmers of blue outlining her hair. Her black nails posed, hands on hips.

Maia moved to keep the lavender sweater swinging—sweat rolling down her sides but no tats or razor scars visible, freckles hidden beneath foundation and powder. Generous eyelashes blinking. *Checklist complete.*

Saucy undressed Maia with a frigid stare. "Well, you'll do. It seems you have some potential at least." Saucy sighed. "Although you're a bit cloddy."

Saucy spun around in a tight circle. "Tomorrow, please wear a white shirt, black skirt, hose, and at least three-inch heels. No dangles."

Maia looked up. "And when can I expect my first paycheck? This is a paid internship, you know."

"Your hair adds something to your look." Her manicured hand zigzagged her tablet. "We'll discuss details when you come tomorrow."

Maia's stilettos poked the icy slush outside the salon. "Paid internships are scarce," she whispered. "The rent will come due soon." She tiptoed past an old toss of scattered gravel. *Picking up towels and sweeping hair in a salon can't be that hard.*

Her lips stiffened. *And spreadsheets fool most economic professors. Especially old white men.*

She smirked and waved her hand for a taxi.

4

Maia started the budget right after breakfast. Her phone buzzed. A text from Tanya.

From the bedroom down the hall.

"It's Jethro, my baby-daddy. He wants to know where I am."

Maia's eyes landed on the last column of numbers. Her fingers entered several more.

Second buzz. "He wants to know if I've had the procedure yet. He says he's gonna kill me if I don't get it done soon."

Maia twisted her lips rightward as she finished the last column of numbers. She let out a long breath. *So much for a budget.*

"Don't tell him where you are," Maia texted.

"He has an app that can trace my cell phone." Tanya's fingers trembled at the message. "He says he's planning to find me today. Even if I hide, he says he'll find me."

Maia looked at the ceiling. Her eyes narrowed. *I used to believe in prayer. Regardless, Tanya could use some help from somebody higher up about now.*

Another text: "And it won't be pretty once he does."

"Disable your phone," Maia texted Tanya. "At least put it in airplane mode. Or take the battery out."

***

Maia texted Shelby. "I have a friend who needs a safe place for a few days. Can she stay with you?"

After ten minutes, Shelby texted back. "Call me."

Maia sighed, her face pouting.

Shelby picked up on the first ring. "Tell me about this friend."

"She's a friend from middle school that I ran into again at college." Maia closed her computer. "You'll remember her. She's a little different."

Maia sighed. "You remember the girl who visited me during my transplant. You know, the bright-pink dress with the enormous bow. She brought her stuffed animal, her brown puppy, with her, even though we were already in middle school."

"Don't remember—that was almost nine years ago. You were twelve then. Why does she need a safe place now?"

"It's a long story. I don't have time for a huge explanation right now."

"Some of your friends aren't the best influence on our kids."

"Well, she won't be at your house long. Just until we can find her a place."

"I can't reach Greg. He must be in a work meeting."

"For God's sake, Shelby, you're a grown woman. You can make your own decisions."

"Okay, then. But your friend will need to come without her phone. And only for ten days. Maximum."

"I'll let her know," Maia replied. "I'll text you when you need to pick her up."

***

Maia texted Tanya. "I've got an out."

She glanced at the front window, then tiptoed into the hall and tapped on Tanya's bedroom door.

"Look," Maia whispered. "I've got a sister who'll give you a place. You'll have to leave your phone here so you can't be traced."

Maia paused. "But I'm warning you. This could be a bit much. She's white, she's a Christian nutcase, and she's into marriage and religion big time."

"Why the hell are you whispering? He ain't here." Tanya followed Maia into the bathroom. "Not yet at least."

Maia grinned, grabbed a lipstick, and arched closer to the mirror. "But my sister lives in a safe part of town, and her husband does target practice for his gun hobby."

"I'm in."

Tanya began stuffing clothes into plastic bags. "This guy's gonna kill me and my baby if he ever finds me. He did time. And he ain't afraid of doin' time again."

* * *

Shelby pulled into the garage in forty minutes. Maia hit the button to close the garage door behind her.

Tanya carried two plastic bags of clothes, one with toiletries poking through the bottom. She wore a mask over her face and a wig over her hair. She climbed into the van, lay across the middle seat, and extended the seat belt. A blanket hid her torso.

"I'm ready," she panted.

"Is your phone with you?"

"No, it's inside. I switched it to airplane mode, if that'll help." Tanya's voice wavered.

Maia hit the garage opener. "I'll get you a burner phone as soon as I can."

Shelby started her van and backed into the street.

Maia yelled after the car, "Tanya, help Shelby if you can. And avoid discussing religion."

The vehicle sped into the morning. Maia's eyes trailed the last glimpse of the sun's glare on the windows, hiding the occupants.

Her shoulders relaxed. She pressed the button to close the garage door and let out a pursed breath. "Unless science is your religion."

5

Maia logged on to her laptop. *No more distractions. Tanya is with Shelby. I need to find an additional job.*

The smell of coffee wafted from the kitchen.

A distant buzz.

Where is Tanya's phone, anyhow? Maia patted the chairs near the table. Then beneath the newspaper on the table. Then the counter. Then the couch.

No phone.

Maybe I can put it in the neighbor's trash. When is his trash day, anyhow? Maybe I can drive it to the nearest Fast Mart—leave it on the ledge outside the outdoor bathroom?

She walked to the kitchen and poured coffee into her favorite mug. *This is crazy. Immature. Not actionable.* She opened the refrigerator to grab some creamer. *Somebody could make this a lot easier—somebody who knows more about phones—somebody who can even make time to research this on the internet.* Stirred the creamer. *A lot less drama, anyhow.*

Maia peeked at the road from the dining room window. A black Dodge was driving slowly past the end of her driveway.

She froze. The lake beyond was a gorgeous blue, the center shimmering with ice. The black Dodge traced the rim, like a black beetle on the rim of a sugar dish.

Maia jerked. *The curtains are open at the dining room window.* She lurched into the hallway to Tanya's bedroom.

The room was disheveled, clothes on the floor, the bathroom counter a chaos of discarded makeup and used eyelashes.

Now is not the time to snoop.

Buzzing. Again. Muffled.

Maia tracked the sound. She dug beneath the clothes, then attacked the bedding. The light from the phone peered through Tanya's pillowcase.

She punched in the remembered passwords. Three messages over the last twenty minutes.

"I'm still waiting."

"You'd better be calling to get an appointment."

"Waiting."

A new buzz: "I'm waiting to hear from you."

Airplane mode won't hide our location. She turned the phone off, then tapped it. *I need to dislodge the battery. But how do you get this thing apart?* Her fingernail popped onto the carpet.

Maia ran to the bathroom and jostled the top drawer. Fingernail clippers clanked as she fumbled to open the phone's battery case. *They aren't strong enough either.* She crouched to the kitchen to find a strong knife.

On the way, she scanned the window. The black Dodge was slowing. Near her driveway.

Another buzz. "I think I can see you. I've found your place."

Maia avoided the window, recoiling down the back stairway, making a straight line to the garage through the basement.

The garage was dark. A small shaft of morning light streamed from under the door. Maia tiptoed to find the jeep door. She eased into the seat.

I don't believe in prayer anymore. But I need that black Dodge to be over the hill when I hit the garage door opener. And I need at least a minute to make it to the street. Her mind headed toward the Fast Mart. *All without being detected.*

She hit the garage door opener and scanned the rearview mirror. The black Dodge was nowhere to be seen. She gunned the jeep in reverse, hit the street, did a quick shift, and sped up toward their small town. She closed the garage door from halfway down the block.

She repressed an urge to toss the phone out a window into the lake. *Foolish. Likely to miss.*

The rearview mirror showed the black Dodge cresting the hill behind her. She managed a quick left. The street abruptly ended in a cul-de-sac. She took a quick breath and corrected with a right turn.

Another buzz: "You need to get this done. Better for us."

Drawbridge ahead. A relic from earlier times. Still working, though. *Could it please open just as I exit the other side?*

The bridge's yellow lights started flashing. But the draw was still down.

Maia gunned the jeep to sixty-five miles per hour. The bells on the bridge started clanging.

She exited the far side. The guards dropped.

Another buzz: "Better for you, especially."

The rearview mirror showed the yellow lights turning red, then the bridge slowly lifting its arms. The ribbon of the river below emerged between its planks. She could also see the black Dodge on the other side, exhaust blowing as the driver revved its engine.

Suddenly, the black Dodge hung a quick left. *There is another bridge seven blocks upstream.*

"Oh, no, you don't!" Maia yelled.

She stepped on the gas and sped by the thirty mile per hour sign. Her eyes scanned to see if the police were around.

An expressway entrance sign. "Take it!" the voice in her head told her.

She sped up to seventy miles per hour on the ramp, then bore straight ahead, racing to a milepost far from the city limits. She pulled into the far-left lane and opened the window. With all the strength her left arm could muster, she threw the cell phone. The rearview mirror showed it bouncing on the grass of the median.

She drove another ten miles, took the exit, and crossed over. No sign of the black Dodge. *Go figure.*

* * *

The black car traced the rim of the lake, then paused at the end of the driveway. Back and forth. Pause. For three days.

Maia bolted the front door and kept the garage door closed. She left the apartment only for classes and her student internship, grabbing groceries when possible, eating leftovers when not.

She kept the curtains closed, peaking between the panels, staring at the end of the driveway. The lake beyond remained icy blue. A hint of green now rimmed the banks.

Maia called Shelby on day six. Yes, Tanya was doing well, no bleeding or problems with the pregnancy. Yes, she'd been a great help. And Tanya had heard from her sister.

Tanya said her sister reported that Jethro had left town, gone out of state. Something about an outstanding warrant for his arrest. Afraid of a traffic stop. Her sister promised to let them know if he came back.

Tanya was ready to move back with Maia. She needed new clothes and to get new extensions in her hair.

6

Dr. Chuck Steinham, chief medical resident, strode into the doctors' lounge, thigh muscles bulging beneath his clinging sweats.

"Just finished seven miles. Unusually warm winter," he announced to the empty ceiling. He slapped his sports towel against his thighs. "Better lunch than cafeteria food!"

He plopped onto the nearest couch and flipped his phone. "No takers. Not yet, anyhow." He grinned. "Nice weekend. Just need some female companionship to complete the itinerary."

Dr. Ben Lawson, third-year resident, kept his back to Steinham. Continued pouring his coffee. Stirred in the creamer. A second dose of creamer. Funneled two packets of sugar into the brew. Grabbed the nearest newspaper, plunked down at the nearest table. Stared at the stock options.

"You should try to arrange your life sometime," Steinham interrupted from his couch.

"Don't have time."

"Well, you need to *make* time. My uncle says you plan for yourself first, and everything else falls into place."

"I thought your uncle only taught you about women."

"Taught me all I needed to know," Steinham chortled, stretching his lanky arms and legs. "Like how to make them fall in love with you when they shouldn't."

"Sounds like you're heading out of town." Ben tasted his coffee. "Must not have a wife or kids."

"No, I don't have kids. And I don't have a wife." Steinham snapped his sweat towel against his thigh again.

"Makes a difference." Ben sipped.

"Wives interrupt your schedule, and kids cost too much money." Steinham propped his foot on the table in front of him. "Kids burp on your clothes until they're two. Then they need pull-ups instead of diapers. You need to start saving for Montessori school, then prom, then college. Then a wedding if they get married." His voice trailed. "You never get finished if you have a kid."

He scrambled to his feet and poked the towel into the waistband of his sweats. "You can always kill a startup if it doesn't make money."

"Good thing you have an engineering degree and not just an MD."

"Yeah, this year's been great. Can't believe this economy. Best sales of informatics software and diagnostic equipment in a decade. I'm up to six employees already."

"Wow." Ben shook his head. "Impressive."

"I love being an entrepreneur! Better than being an Attending." Steinham glanced around the doctors' lounge and lowered his voice. "If you stay here, you'll always be an employee, somebody else's lackey. No matter how many degrees you get or how hard you work."

Ben nodded again. "Yep, creativity pays off." Another sip. "But how do you keep up with the medical literature?"

Steinham checked his phone again. He chuckled.

Dr. Charlie Lee, another third-year resident, raced through the lounge and grabbed a sealed sandwich from the refrigerator. The door slammed after him.

Ben gulped the last of his cold coffee. He landed his cup in the garbage on the first throw, then punched the same door bar to the stairwell.

***

"Oh, to have a brain like Steinham. At least three college degrees."

Ben listened to the door latch behind him. "And to have his money, his family connections." *His courage. His sense of adventure. His willingness to plan.*

He sighed and started up the stairs.

Just one weekend away.

Five more flights to go. *An alternative to the gym.*

Yes, Ben had a family. A dad.

A good man, a family man, Ben reminded himself. *A dad with no remarkable awards, never climbed a mountain, never reduced his golf handicap of twenty-five.*

Ben paused, breathing hard. *I don't remember if Dad ever golfed much. He was a steady man, an employee.*

He paused again at the next landing. *Never an entrepreneur.*

He looked up to the sound of footsteps. Dr. Chin Zu Zhia, research affiliate, heading down the stairs.

"Sorry to hear you're leaving." Ben paused to catch his breath.

"Well, the virus is spreading." Dr. Zhia continued down.

"You're not on any lockdown yet."

"My family video calls from China every day. They worried. They on lockdown. Seventeen cities locked down."

"But it's only January 23. You told me your medical school is over 500 kilometers from the epicenter of the new virus."

"My family say I need to leave while flights still operate."

"Well, the best to you. I'll miss you."

"Miss you too. My medical school will be in lockdown for another five weeks. At least until early March. I may have time to connect online."

Dr. Zhia continued down, his steps getting fainter. Ben headed up another flight.

"I wonder if I'll ever see him again. Nice guy."

7

Dusk hesitated outside the window. The trees lifted their scrawny arms in black silhouette above the lingering snow of the early February storm. Lights popped brightly in the skyscrapers across the water.

The windowpane reflected a seated doctor, a stethoscope in the pocket of his white lab coat, computer tablet opened on the counter.

Dr. Ben Lawson, medical resident, stepped softly into the space next to Dr. Clarke.

"What do you mean you 'just called?'" Dr. Ed Clarke's pitch rose, his tone snide. "You never call unless you need something." He tapped the counter with the blunt end of his pen.

Dr. Ben blinked, his eyes tracking to the receiver in Dr. Clarke's ear.

Pause.

Bits of scrambled conversation.

"What is it this time? A party with your friends? An afternoon at the spa? New hair extensions?"

Dr. Ben Lawson cleared his throat. "For your signature," he whispered, placing the documents in front of Dr. Clarke, pen in writing position. *For the Attending Physician.*

A pause. The earpiece leaked—the other party pleading.

"Well, be quick about it. I have work to do." Dr. Clarke grabbed the pen. "Patients to see," he growled.

The wheels of the rolling stool scraped grit as Dr. Clarke adjusted his weight toward Ben. "Entitled brats!" he huffed. "My family always thinking I'm available to solve their problems."

Dr. Clarke abruptly stood, his white lab coat falling into starched pleats despite the early evening. "More money, more decisions." His stethoscope dangled. "As if the money I deposit every month isn't enough."

He kicked the rolling stool under the counter. "The officials say a virus is heading this way from China. And now my daughter calls! She wants me to meet her."

He turned to Dr. Ben, holding the documents suspended in signature position. "Aren't these forms online yet?"

Dr. Ben breathed slowly. "They need a hard copy with the Attending Physician's signature for Mr. Smith's work."

Dr. Clarke flipped through the thirteen pages. "I see that your handwriting is still legible."

Silence.

"I don't recall this man." Dr. Clarke slammed the packet on the counter but picked up the pen.

"Mr. Smith is the dock worker who fell on the subway stairs and got a superficial femoral blood clot in his thigh, then a pulmonary embolism. He claims he's still short of breath and has swelling in his legs." Ben's voice thinned. "So I gave him an extra five days off work. He's seeing his primary doctor in three days to get his medications adjusted."

Dr. Clarke held the pen in midair. "Lawson, have you ever loaded a barge on the dock?"

"No, sir. I went straight from high school to four years of college, to four years of medical school, to internship and residency." Dr. Ben paused. "I've been here four years."

The furnace vent grumbled, then blew warm air.

Ben stiffened. "I clerked at the courthouse to earn money during college."

Dr. Ed Clarke raised one eyebrow and laid a heavy signature on the last page.

Dr. Ben captured the document, grabbed the pen, and hurried out the door. Halfway down the hall, he let out a breath and shook his head. "This Attending Physician is supposed to write me letters of recommendation next year?"

8

"Can't take three minutes for his own daughter?" Maia hissed. "Like I want more of his money!" She tapped the red button at the bottom of the blurry screen. She wicked tears from the outer creases of her eyes and sniffled. Loudly.

"What I really want is ninety seconds of his time! Undivided by his blasted phone." She attacked the buttons on her coat. "Like, to discuss college courses, potential career choices."

Maia flung her scarf around her neck, then took a swallow from her water bottle.

"It doesn't matter," she whispered, her face dropping. *It hasn't mattered. Not since he left, at least.*

She took another swig from the water bottle. *Cold, almost icy.* "Maybe it never did."

She straightened her shoulders and strutted from the Student Union into the spitting cold. The wind caught her umbrella, twisting its form, the scarf slapping her face. Her angry boots echoed on the cold sidewalk, the dim lightbulb fading after the first twenty feet.

The rusty frame of the bus shelter groaned in the wind. She plunked onto the frigid metal bench inside. "Positive thoughts," she scolded. "Maybe my dad's God will make him love me." Scattered sleet landed on her boots. "Fat chance."

She peered through the dirty glass at the lanes of traffic braking for the light on the corner. *Must still be rush hour. The bus is likely to be late. Maybe I should have taken the subway?*

She stood, wrapped her scarf closer around her neck and stomped circulation into her feet. *But a little more money to pay bills would really help about now. Especially if this virus turns out to be more than a rumor.*

Maia pinched the tip of her gloves between her teeth, pulled them off, and shook out their sleet. Her fingers dialed Sonja. No answer. *Likely having dinner with her family—always leaves the phone in the next room.* "Prissy!" Maia dramatized. The frigid solitude of the bus shelter shuddered in the wind.

She scanned her Favorites and groaned. Clarisse just started a new venture firm in Asia. *Notable time difference.* Nadia was in Europe, supposedly studying art. *More likely sipping champagne with some hot French guy on her parents' credit card.* Maia tapped her phone for the ever-student Kim Lee: *voice mail.*

A buzz.

"Hey, Princess," the chat clamored. "When ya going to show more online? We've seen more than your white thighs before!"

"A customer?" *Don't they know I have a life?* Maia pressed her lips together. *My work at the club is just a job, a way to raise money fast.*

She punched another favorite number and sat down. *The frigid bench again.*

"I wish I knew which pronoun you wanted me to use today, brother dear," she whispered away from the phone. "After all, you've been transitioning for two years now."

* * *

"Hi, Dana," Maia started tentatively. She glimpsed at her rings and the bracelets on her wrists. *Dana isn't wearing these today.* She twisted her neck to see her reflection in the muddied glass. And she wasn't sharing her makeup. *Another benefit to living in your own apartment.*

"Hi," said Dana, the voice sullen.

"I just wanted to know you were okay," she stammered. "Have you heard about the new virus?"

"Don't know anyone who has it."

"Well, it's not like we can't still see each other," she offered.

"That's not likely. Mom said if this virus threatens students, and the mayor closes the schools, Professor Rasheed may have to share their office at home and teach his university classes online."

"I doubt the virus will get that bad. Besides, university students are required to be fully vaccinated. They're young and healthy."

Dana paused. "The house already feels crowded. I doubt Mom would be happy to see you."

"Well, if I don't get paid by the time the rent is due, she'll have to get over herself. I'm coming home," Maia asserted. "There's a couch in the den that will work just fine."

"I thought you were *essential*," Dana chided, the pitch of the voice noticeably higher. "You should be able to keep working."

"I *am* essential," she retorted. "The new use of this term is irksome already. Everybody is essential, regardless of what rules the bureaucrats make."

"Yeah, like men at the club still have their needs." Dana's voice dripped sarcasm.

"Maybe they can slip the mayor a little extra."

"Fortunately, I haven't had to address those needs yet." Maia stiffened. "Everybody gives their time and bodies to something." She sniffed. "Some people just get paid more than others."

Dana went quiet.

"Are you still there?" Maia spoke again. "I hope this new virus doesn't spread and delay your reassignment surgery."

"Doesn't matter," Dana retorted.

"Well, it's already February. You need to call that sperm bank and store some. In case you change your mind later and want kids."

"I don't want kids. Not now. Not ever."

"Well, you might change your mind," Maia cautioned. "Speaking of kids, is Shelby still planning Easter at her house this year?"

"Oh, yeah, she is planning, I'm pretty sure. With all her people."

Maia noticed yellow flashing lights heading her way, the head beams reflecting on the slants of rain.

"That discussion will have to wait. The bus is coming, and it's too noisy to hear you." Maia fingered her gloves. "Besides, Easter isn't until April 12 this year. We have almost two months to figure this out."

"Seems to me you should want to see her. After all, she gave you cells for your transplant."

"As long as her stem cells stay out of my brain."

Maia punched the red button.

Couch surfing is not for sissies.

9

I am sinister, a pretender. Devious, even demonic.

I am the spiny creature in the closet lurking to find you when you least suspect me. Hiding, I disrupt systems. I spew cytokines. I make clots where none should be. I kill doctors, patients, and dreams.

I am rearranging the futures of all creatures, not just those I infect.

10

The bus chugged through the streets, litter hugging the smoky patches of old snow, its belly swaying to miss the potholes.

Jakeem Robert plopped close to the middle door. He checked inside his coat and felt the plastic badge. He flipped out his ID and stared at it.

Jakeem Robert. His name. Momma said his father's name was Robert. *Never met the man.*

The bus lumbered past blocks of plywood-boarded buildings. He passed the house of Sherise, his first love. A tingle of delight fused his cheeks. Then, the house of Keyla, a nice tart, maybe too nice. Then, the house of Cherika. He peered out the window to see signs of light. None yet. She might not be home from work. *Wonder if she's still shacked up with that guy?* His mind evoked the guy with the backward cap and the gang tats. *Wonder if he still be in the hood?*

He really missed Cherika; and Jada, his daughter. He pulled back from the glass, a sad face reflecting in the window. *No man should miss his woman this much.*

And he couldn't keep his promise to himself to be a good dad to the kid, if the judge said no.

The graffiti became familiar. The yellow house came into view. Yellow with white porch pillars, looking stately-like from yester-time. Granny had lived here since he could remember. A good woman. Steady-like.

The bus lurched into a pothole, splashing rain from the night before onto the people waiting beside the strips of snow. The centerfold door moaned.

Jakeem rolled out.

The neighbor's dog started howling at the bus and running laps on their side of the fence, frothing and drooling.

Jakeem ambled up the sidewalk, scanning for cracks and patches of ice that gleamed in the dimming light.

The dog beast paused his running to snarl, then lurch against the rusty links.

Chains clanked. Bits of ice flew.

Jakeem lifted his wrist, his watch glinting in the sunset.

Granny will surely hear the rattling and howling.

But the place stayed dark.

Jakeem shivered and stomped his feet. Then he rapped on the peeling paint of the screen door, staying clear of the ragged screen. *Don't need no bleedin' now. Need to keep this CNA uniform clean.*

He bent his head, his right ear toward the house. Slippers shuffling, getting closer, the place still dark. *Must be savin' on the 'lectric bill.*

The porch light popped on. Jakeem stepped back, his mouth contorting at the creak of the slats.

"Well, I'll be," Granny's round face chirped. Her hair was still capped, kitchen sneakin' out. He grunted at food stains on her wrinkled robe. *A very long night or a very short day.*

Jakeem stepped inside, careful of that knife-like screen, ignoring the moan of the hinges. He steadied his nose and swallowed. *Burned grease and stale clothes.*

The door banged behind him. The last vestiges of sunlight danced on specks of dust. His eyes adjusted. Clothes littered the two sagging couches that hogged the middle of the room. An unmade bed hid in the corner.

He unzipped his coat.

Granny ranted nonstop. She claimed the gangbangers been at it last night, shootin' until three in the mornin'. Never mind the cold and the rain. She could hardly sleep at all, and sleeping in the bathtub didn't sound warm enough. Granny would risk the bullets with one ear open. Or so she said.

Jakeem shifted his leg. A board beneath the carpet creaked.

Granny finally looked at him. "Well, boy, what brings you here? You need some eats?"

"Naw" He shuffled. He pulled a crumpled envelope from his pants pocket. "One hundred-eighty dolla', Gran. That be it. Short week at work. All of February, they say this new virus causin' crib."

Granny took the envelope and counted the bills.

"Well, I thanks thee kindly." Her voice turned all business-like. "That landman wants his rent—ain't been too keen on me bein' late fir his pay."

Jakeem turned to leave. *Granny will expect a hug.* He cleared his throat.

"Hey, Granny, the bangers have a new sign for *out.*"

He bumped her elbow, then charged through the front room. The main door slammed, then the screen door slapped behind him.

* * *

Jakeem badged into the rehabilitation and nursing facility at 7:23 p.m. *Dark already.* He banged the slush and water from his treads inside the employee entry. Then he attacked the gear: the disposable gown, the shoe covers, the hair cover, the mask. *More and more, every day. But a CNA has to wear this stuff.*

Someday, this will be goggles!

He turned on the water to wash his hands. He held up his hands to dry, then gingerly tugged on the gloves. *As the instructor said.*

All for this crib virus. But I don't want to catch the thing. This virus does mean things, especially to black brothers. I don't want to die.

He squinted in the mirror above the sink. *Not yet, anyhow.*

Jakeem headed down the hall. The floors reeked of chlorine and shone with wax. White fluorescent bulbs buzzed in the ceiling. *Reflectin' nicely.*

He pumped his mind. *I need to speak with proper English.* He pasted a smile below his mask, hoping his eyes smiled too.

"Good afternoon, Miss Bates," he greeted the lead nurse.

He shushed the voice in his head. *Ain't no black man supposed to be takin' no orders from no white wo-man! No way!*

He forced a smile. *Miss Bates likely been at this place longer than I been alive. And I need more bread than chips. It's time for the eyes to lie.*

"Three new admissions today," Miss Bates announced. "More coming tomorrow, the director says, if a bed opens up. This virus is keeping them sick long enough to need rehab."

Jakeem studied the patient roster: full. *Miss Bates never starts slow.*

"I've beat many white boys," he hid a deep breath and whispered into his mask. "I wonder if I can beat this China virus."

11

Maia plugged in her laptop. She dusted the glistening logo. *A bite out of an apple. Opinion unchanged since Eden.* She lifted the lid, hit the start button, and waited for the crescendo wheeze.

The news declared that as of March 16, 2020, the university would close for in-person classes. *Today is March 3. That's less than two weeks away.* Classes were to be online, professors to adapt to online curricula. Research papers were still due, online, at the previously scheduled times.

The mayor was closing all nonessential businesses in two weeks—*March 23, to be exact.*

Yesterday, a long-standing employee from Fuchsia Salon packed a travel case with minimum inventory, advertising house calls—shampoos, colorings, nails, and massages. All in the home. And with masks worn, if the customer preferred.

She was starting solo. She hadn't invited Maia to come along.

Well, at least I can harvest her ideas for the econ paper. "Adaptability as a Marker of Economic Resilience

During Uncertain Times," complete with pie charts. *That professor, old white buzzard that he is, will be too busy gearing up for online teaching to fact-check the data.*

Maia clicked on her application for a job in home delivery services. *Seems promising. People are already hiding in their homes, fearful of themselves, their own families and their coworkers.*

Three days ago, she had contacted Matt, her physical trainer. She needed him to help her get buff for the seventy-pound lifting required by this job. He reminded her the gym was considered a nonessential business and would close March 23. Given the time constraints, he advised her to research the internet for home exercises. *Already done that. Boxes of books weighed on a bathroom scale? Really? Carrying these up and down stairs in your apartment building with a mask on? Are they kidding?*

No word yet from her initial test for the virus. This new job required every employee to be tested twice a week. *Unclear if this will help limit spread of the virus, but the benefits package offsets the pay.*

* * *

A text from the delivery company. "Your test for coronavirus is positive."

"Hey, Tanya. Guess what?" Maia stood to stretch. "That delivery company says my coronavirus test is positive."

"All the more reason to end this pregnancy." Tanya padded to the refrigerator and opened its door. "The lady on TV said they don't know if this virus will harm the baby or not. This virus is too new to tell."

Maia joined her in the kitchen. "Don't know if you'll find what you want in there. There must have been a run on the stores." Maia steamed her tea pod in her cup on the counter. "Panicked people, I guess. Couldn't find what I usually buy. In fact, a lot of the shelves were empty."

Tanya opened a carton of yogurt. "Just wait 'til the state learns you've had a stem cell transplant." She licked her spoon. "Let alone that you're the roommate/landlord of a pregnant person."

"Well, they say I need to isolate for fourteen days. I have no symptoms, just a positive test." Maia grabbed a random pen from the counter.

Who came up with that magic number? Let's see. I had the test five days ago. Nine days to go. Nine days with no income. And the rent is still due at the end of the month.

"Tanya, the rent is due on the thirty-first. Since you're staying here now, have you considered paying half?"

"I'll need to contact my social worker. That may be a problem."

Maia punched her phone for the club. "Say, Monesto, are you short any dancers for Saturday night?"

He hacked. *Cigarettes.* Then the horn of him blowing his nose. "One girl called in last night. She's scheduled for Saturday, but I don't know if she'll show. You might as well be here. I may need you on the pole."

Eleven days. Not sick. Close enough.

"I'll be there."

12

The wind howled through the three sides of the tent. *To limit the risk of infection. Or so the C-suite says.*

Gusts of wind stretched the ties. The pegs groaned to hold on. Fifty-three degrees with intermittent rain.

Dr. Ben Lawson shivered. He phoned Dr. Charlie Lee.

"Brr! It's cold in here. I'm even wishing I could do jumping jacks to keep warm."

"Well, you can't do that. The patients will see you." Charlie chuckled. "Just think, it's March 13. You're almost halfway through another day. And it's only two and a half more weeks before the rotation change."

"It can't come soon enough, from my perspective."

"Come on! It's an unusually warm winter. For New York, that is."

"But I haven't been this cold since I forgot to pay my utility bill during medical school boards five years ago." Dr. Ben's teeth chattered into the phone. "Did they ever update the hospital memo?"

Charlie's foam cup hit the trash can, tin echoing through the phone. "Nope. The C-suite still claims that screening in the tent should spare others from the new virus. Hey, take one for the team."

Ben adjusted his mask and rubbed his foggy glasses on his coat sleeve. "Say, I thought these N95 masks were just for laminar airflow rooms. At the last fitting, they gave us strict instructions these didn't work for viruses, only to limit TB and possibly respiratory MRSA."

"At least it's something. They say it's all we have." Charlie chortled. "At least the gown and gloves save some heat."

Ben stamped his feet on the asphalt. *Warm and ready.* "Have you been home yet, Charlie?"

"Nope, not yet."

"Well, I hoped that staying at the hotel would spare my family exposure to this new virus. But boxed cereal with cold milk is still a cold meal. And microwaved eggs and bitter coffee are getting old." Ben hugged his coat around his neck.

"This must be affecting me. I'm even missing the tourists!"

"Yeah, but my wife hasn't been answering my texts or phone calls lately. Her messages are pretty cryptic." Ben blew warm breath into his hands. "I have no idea what my kids are doing. I haven't thought of anything other than this cursed place and all these sick people for days."

"Well, I don't have any kids yet." Charlie sighed.

Dr. Ben heard the nurse from the other side of the tent wall. "The doctor will see you now."

He stamped his feet again and plastered a smile on his face. "Got to let you go, Charlie. Duty calls."

"Did you see the magnolia tree outside the tent?" Charlie rushed. "Bursting. Full white. At least something is beautiful, hopeful."

"Gotta go, Charlie."

"Yeah, I know you've got to go. But maybe the blossoming trees can cheer you—at least they aren't moving to stay warm like you are."

***

The rain stopped mid-morning and the wind slowed as the afternoon progressed. Droves of patients descended upon the tent. *Not much to offer them. Hospitalization or nothing. They have a virus, after all! Why don't they just stay home?*

Dr. Ben shrugged beneath the yellow gown covering his white lab coat. *Perhaps a nebulizer? A note for their boss?*

***

Dr. Ben Lawson watched the nurse lead the next patient behind the shaky divider: a woman holding onto the hand of a small girl. The little girl had a smudgy face, stringy hair, no socks, and oversized, scruffy boys' shoes. She dutifully helped the panting lady onto a plastic chair.

The nurse handed Dr. Ben the chart, covertly pointing to Spanish as the preferred language. "The older lady is the patient; the child is the granddaughter," she whispered. "Isabella Zapota, age forty-eight. Fever for four days. She wants a note to show her landlord in case she misses work and doesn't get paid."

The low howl of the wind skirted the divider.

Dr. Ben Lawson looked at the lady. Determination and fear blazed from Isabella's near-black eyes.

"Buenas tardes, señora. ¿Cómo está?"

Dr. Ben sat across from the woman. He noticed Isabella's deep-brown eyes now registered relief. She blurted her story quickly. In Spanish. She hadn't been able to smell the garbage outside her apartment or taste jalapeños for almost a week. A fever started four days ago with a cough and sore throat. The diarrhea started then, with aching in her joints. Her toes turned bluish yesterday. She was so short of breath and so tired, she could barely get her work done. Yes, someone at her job had the new virus, but she didn't work with them. If she could just have a few days off work, she would improve.

Dr. Ben moved the divider to limit the draft. The lady had red conjunctivae, dusky fingers. Isabella nodded that he could lift her blouse. Her lungs were clear, her heart fast but regular without murmurs, her belly soft, her skin without rash. Dr. Lawson stared at the vital signs: temperature 103.4, respiratory rate 28, pulse oximetry 89%.

His phone vibrated. He stole a glance at the screen. The hospital chief medical officer. "Limit personal protective gear to those intubating patients in ICUs. Gear and ventilators scarce. More patients expected."

"No health insurance. She doesn't want a chest x-ray," the nurse whispered from the side.

"Sadly fortunate," Dr. Ben muttered. He glanced at the nurse and the electronic scribe typing at the computer. "This virus often shows infiltrates on chest x-rays. We don't know if we should treat these or not."

His eyes examined Isabella again. *But by day eight, they warn, this can become deadly.*

"Listen, I need some help with the Spanish here," he pleaded to the nurse. "Tell her I need to admit her to the hospital for a few days. Promise her we'll involve a social worker early to help her with any costs related to her care."

The nurse started in Spanish. Isabella began protesting with her hands.

"She refuses," the nurse informed Ben. "She has no one to watch the child. She promises she'll come back if she gets worse."

The child lifted Isabella's hand as they headed out of the tent. The nurse wrinkled her forehead above her mask.

"Right now, she intends to go home."

* * *

The sun crept behind the buildings. Dr. Ben Lawson's phone said 5:50 p.m. He tore off his stethoscope, twisted it into his pocket, and looked for his replacement MD. He headed to the hospital, his shoes squishing in the water-logged gravel. Warm air spewed from the ceiling vent above the entrance.

He paused in the doorway, scraping muddy grit off his shoes. A brigade of newly minted medical personnel barraged him with questions. "Did he have any symptoms of the new virus? Did he have a fever? Had he been exposed to anyone diagnosed with the new virus?" Dr. Ben smirked. *Who knows what laboratory test will define this illness?*

He tracked to the doctors' lounge.

Dr. Steinham was already there, feet propped on a coffee table. "Say, isn't it great to be involved in something from the ground up?"

"That important, eh?"

"Experts are flying here from all over the world to sort this out." Steinham clucked. "Those public health and epidemiology courses are finally paying off!"

Ben headed to the refrigerator, his movements tracked by the reflection in the window. *It's gotten dark. That lady and her granddaughter must be heading to the bus about now.*

"Hey, Dr. Steinham, I saw a lady whose condition worries me." Ben slammed the refrigerator door. "Today, in the tent."

Steinham didn't look up. "Well, I'm not worried. I'll be out of here soon enough."

Ben plodded, empty-handed, to his mailbox and extracted an envelope.

"Say, my wife is writing to me." He waved the envelope.

Silence.

Ben's lips torqued left. *This is one way to reach me.*

Steinham continued to scroll on his phone.

"This was postmarked March 8, 2020," Ben grumbled. "We've been here a while."

Steinham's fingers pawed the screen.

Ben stared at the large, erratic script.

"If you stay at that hospital one more night, the kids and I are leaving for Florida. You can stay there and die with those people if they mean more to you than we do. But my folks have room, and at least I'll have an adult to talk to!"

Laura—sloppy, bold signature. Almost unrecognizable.

Ben stepped inside a dictation room and hit her speed dial. Her phone went to voicemail. Before he could leave a message, the overhead crackled.

"Rapid Response, ICU!"

Steinham jumped to the door. It banged shut after him.

"I'm coming," Ben yelled after Steinham. He limped to the door. "Old soccer injury," he sputtered. "I can't do this forever."

13

The wind snatched Isabella's mask as she stepped off the bus. She scurried to the outside of the crowd. The girl child followed closely, eyes wide, quiet.

"No elevador, mi amor," The older woman whispered in Spanish. She herded the child toward the stairs. "People don't want to catch what I've got."

Isabella rested halfway up each flight of stairs. She handed the little girl her purse. Beads of sweat trickled down her forehead, flickering in the dim light. She pushed back her scarf and gasped for air. "Only a few more feet."

Gabriela caught the door on the third-floor landing and wedged her tiny body to hold it open. She rummaged through Isabella's purse for the key, used it, then put it in her own coat pocket.

Inside, Isabella held onto a kitchen chair, catching her breath.

"Gabriela, heat the rice and beans."

Isabella lurched toward the bedroom. "Let me know when the food is ready," she whispered in Spanish.

* * *

Twenty minutes passed. "Abuelita, el arroz y frijoles."

No answer.

"Grandma, the rice and beans are getting cold," Gabriela called again.

Gabriela went into the single bedroom.

Isabella lay face down across the double bed.

Gabriela patted her shoulder. "The rice and beans are still warm."

Isabella moaned. *She is sleeping a very hard sleep.*

Gabriela touched Grandma's skin. *Doesn't look the right color.*

She squeezed her abuelita's limp hand. Harder and harder. *Abuelita doesn't try to push me away or make me stop.*

Gabriela looked at her fist. *But Grandma says I shouldn't hit anybody.*

She smacked Abuelita in the shoulder with her child-soggy fist. Another moan. She looked at her fist again, her forehead wrinkled.

Gabriela pushed the bottom button of the lock on their apartment door and ran three doors down. There, the neighbors spoke a language she could understand. *Abuelita says they just got here from Venezuela.* She pounded on their door. No answer.

She ran back to the kitchen, grabbed Abuelita's purse, and dug for their cell phone.

They said in school to hit the E button if I ever needed help.

The 911 operator answered. In English. Many questions.

She threw the cell phone back into Grandma's purse and stood close to the wall.

Gabriela heard sirens coming closer. She heard the elevator open and loud voices and boots heading toward them.

Men in space suits entered the apartment.

The lady from Venezuela came from down the hall. She stepped inside and looked around.

The men in space suits put Grandma on a stretcher and hooked a tube in her nose. Gabriela backed closer against the wall.

Those men fastened the straps to hold Abuelita. They tossed her purse on top of the straps.

Halfway out the door, one man turned to Gabriela. "Where are you going to spend tonight, little girl?"

Gabriela's lower lip trembled. "I sleep there." She pointed to the couch.

The man furrowed his eyebrows.

Gabriela straightened her shoulders and stretched to be all of her almost six years.

"Can't I just stay here? Grandma always gets back from her other job before the big clock outside strikes midnight."

A buzz from their cell phone. The first man eyed it. He nodded to the second man in the space suit. "Call CPS. See if they'll answer this late."

The men whisked Abuelita's stretcher toward the door. "Gotta go. Another run ten blocks down."

The second man muttered into his mask. "I called CPS twice and left a message. They haven't answered yet."

The neighbor from Venezuela tiptoed back to her apartment.

Gabriela locked the door. *I've never spent the whole night all by myself.*

She stared at the rice and beans still on the table, then moved to scarf down her food and put Abuelita's plate in the refrigerator. She climbed on a chair to rinse the dishes in the sink. *The cockroaches won't have a fiesta while Abuelita is gone.*

Gabriela grabbed her blanket from the bed and snuggled into the familiar front couch to wait. The streetlight cast shadows through the window onto the wall.

"Abuelita will be back soon," she whispered as she pulled the blanket up to her chin. "Before the big clock outside strikes midnight."

14

The stretcher rolled into the sudden bright lights of the intensive care unit. Isabella's face winced.

Dr. Ashraff surveyed the immobile body strapped to the stretcher.

"Do you ever wonder if these people even remember the ambulance ride or their time in the ER?" he quizzed the respiratory therapist as they moved the moaning body from the stretcher to the bed.

"I don't know." The therapist tightened the straps, adjusted the light again, and hit the pedal. The bed rolled Isabella onto her stomach. "But this one seems to float between Heaven and Earth. And I'm not just talking about proning."

Dr. Ashraf fixed his eyes on the oxygen monitor. "If you believe in that sort of thing."

The oxygen monitor showed a line trending downward.

"We need to intubate this lady."

Dr. Ashraf adjusted his mask and opened two pairs of sterile gloves side by side on the counter, then stepped to the sink. He watched the water dribble down his fingers. He flicked away the water and held up his hands. Dry enough to double glove.

"It's a good thing you're good at intubations." The respiratory therapist gathered sedatives, instruments, and the tube. "You always get it on the first try."

Dr. Ashraf's eyes reviewed the instruments. "Well, I'm getting lots of practice." He glanced at the name above the bed: "Isabella Zapota."

Dr. Ashraf paused by the bedside screen: pulse oximetry of 65%, blood pressure of 70/diastolic, pulse racing at 130. He muttered into his mask. "I wonder if being such a star at this procedure was worth all the accolades during training. I wonder how many of us are going to die of this virus while trying to help the poor wretches who already have it."

The respiratory therapist advanced the instruments toward him on the tray.

Dr. Ashraf surveyed the petite form in front of him. She had red skin, but her blue toes protruded from the white sheet. He watched intently. *She is not moving her right side.*

He turned to the newly arrived nurse. "What is this lady's Glasgow Coma Scale?"

"Below eight."

"Another reason to intubate. Did she sign a consent?"

"A consent?" The nurse shook her head. "No family came with her."

"Well, let's get this done. If she stands a chance to live, she needs a stable airway."

He picked up a small, curved blade and shortened the stylet. He nodded to the respiratory therapist, then tipped the jaw and peaked down the throat. "Unusually red. Very swollen," he whispered. "No bougie with this one. Avoid any risk of spasm." Dr. Ashraf held his breath, steam hitting his glasses above his mask.

"Gently, gently through those vocal cords."

He straightened his back. "Made it." He held the tube with one hand, reaching with the other. "End-tidal CO2 monitor?"

The therapist handed him the monitor, then a device to secure the tube. He secured the tube, then walked over to the ventilator.

"Every one of these ventilators is different," he complained.

The nurse scrolled the computer. "The best we can do, given the situation."

"Her peak pressures are high," he reminded the backs of the nurse and the therapist. "Stiff lungs—not the best." He fumbled with the buttons on the ventilator, his eyes glued to the dials.

"Does she have any labs back yet?" *Not that we know what any of these labs mean. New virus and all.*

"Her creatinine is 4.5, bicarb 16, chloride and potassium low, sodium 135." The nurse wrinkled her forehead above her mask. "Her hemoglobin is okay, but the platelets are low. The d-dimer and CRP are high."

"And what is her APACHE score?"

"Climbing. It was lower when she came in."

"Call the intensivists. I'm an anesthesiologist." Dr. Ashraf headed for the door. "I've put in enough ventilator orders until they get here."

"Don't forget to discard your protective equipment," the therapist reminded him. "There's a receptacle outside the room."

"Yeah." He nodded. "For now, we can discard this stuff."

Dr. Ashraf made the hall before he tore off his gown and the gloves in one motion. The wad hit the trash. "Soon we'll be squirreling it away because we don't have any left."

He yelled back to the nurse, "I'll put my note in the computer from the OR."

The door swung wildly, then slammed shut.

He started walking. *Healthier, elective surgery patients need an anesthesiologist. Enough of this getting roped out of the operating room to intubate patients in the ICU.* He turned left toward the operating suite.

He passed a urologist, an orthopedist, and an expedited medical student headed to the ICU. Presumably, to recall internal medicine, pulmonary care, and ventilator management from their remote memory. From medical school. From after their third set of board exams.

He kept his eyes focused on the posters on the wall.

15

Dr. Ben Lawson made it from the hotel to the hospital by 6:50 a.m. He felt better. He still hadn't heard from his wife or his kids. Although he had tried several times.

But he had slept, his breakfast had included waffles, and the coffee had been hot.

He nodded gratitude for the shoe covers, the mask, the gown, and two pairs of gloves. He backed into the first room in the ICU.

The sign-out on this one was brief: a new patient, came in by ambulance, brought to ICU, and intubated last night. No family with her.

"No family has called yet this morning." A nurse's voice came from the darkness surrounding the computer screen.

"Well, no family is allowed in person, anyhow. Not since this virus."

He noticed the name above the bed: "Isabella Zapota." A haunt. *I saw this lady in the tent yesterday afternoon. So much for hospital duties today.*

"You could try to reach somebody in her family," he instructed the nurse.

Isabella's moist curls framed her dark face. White tape hid most of her upturned nose. An orograstric tube deformed her mouth. Her tiny frame looked even smaller in a hospital bed.

A phone rang in the patient's closet.

Dr. Ben curved his gloved hand to improvise a reflex mallet. Normal on the left. *Brisk reflexes on the right.*

He rubbed her sternum through her gown. Her left side responded; her right didn't move. He scrolled his computer and ordered a head CT. "Evaluate for stroke." *No need to make this STAT. We've likely missed the window for stroke intervention. Who knows how many hours she has been this way?*

The nurse turned from her computer. "You understand this lady is number eight on the list? CTs of the chest, not the head, are the priority for this virus. And we have to take precautions, so everything is taking longer."

Dr. Ben nodded and turned to the medications ordered by the intensivist. Heparin, a steroid, hydroxychloroquine, zinc, azithromycin. *It's amazing what is ordered. Old drugs, exploited side-effects. No randomized-controlled trials, no protocols yet. Clinical experience? Best guesses?*

The bedside monitor dinged. Blood pressure 70/ diastolic.

The nurse scanned the computer: "Her creatinine increased from 4 to 6, her bicarb dropped from 16 to 11."

Dr. Ben keyboarded quickly. "Renal consultant to please see patient and advise."

He spoke to the nurse. "I'm ordering a dopamine drip for the blood pressure and a nephrology consult. Hopefully, the dopamine will help the kidneys. If we can improve the low blood pressure, maybe they can still try CRRT."

* * *

Moisture dripped from the awning above the window. Gabriela's eyelids fluttered in the light of the morning sun. She wriggled her toes back under the blanket and snuggled into the warmth of the couch. She listened to the ticking of the kitchen clock.

Suddenly, she lifted her head, alert.

"Didn't Abuelita come home last night?"

She plunged off the couch and ran to the bedroom. Only a made bed. *Didn't Abuelita sleep in the bed last night*?

Gabriela went back into the big room, squinting in the warm brightness of the sun beaming through the window.

She fingered her lower lip. *Abuelita was sick, and those men in space suits came and took her away.*

A roach darted across the floor to a newspaper in the corner. *I wonder where they took her*?

The roach circled back to the sunlight, then raced to hide between the pages.

Where did she go?

Her tummy growled. She tiptoed to the refrigerator and wedged open the door. The light flickered. Tortillas, beans, rice, hot sauce, jalapeños. She rubbed her eyes. *How does Abuelita make those?*

Chair scraping, plates clattering, microwave pings.

She downed the cooling food and wiped the crumbs off the table. *No fiesta for the roaches. Just like Abuelita says.*

Gabriela walked back to the warmth of the sunlight streaming through the window and gazed down at the sidewalk below. *There are no people on the street down there.*

A gasped breath. *Did I miss school?*

Her eyes scanned to a school bag hanging on its hook by the door. *Or is it not happening again?*

She ran to the bedroom, the bed still made, the covers rumpled. *That's where Abuelita was before the spacemen took her.*

Gabriela tugged their one suitcase from under the bed and pulled out a plaid skirt, then dumped the contents onto the floor. A rumpled yellow blouse fell from the bottom. She put on the yellow blouse and the plaid skirt, then grabbed her shoes and spread her toes into their wideness. She smiled at the scruffs on the toes. *That boy down the hall must really be big now. His mom was so nice to give them to us.*

Gabriela stood, examining herself in the mirror on the back of the door. Her face gleamed.

She opened the front door to the hall and counted three doors down. *They will understand me when I talk.* Gabriela ran down the hall and pounded on the door.

No answer. *Maybe my hand isn't strong enough?*

A really black lady poked a turbaned head out her door. She glared at Gabriela in the hall. Then she yelled at someone behind her. *Some strange language.* Gabriela lowered her head and ran back to her apartment, slammed the door, and locked it.

She stood with her back against the door, held her breath, and listened.

No footsteps.

Gabriela rummaged through the pile from the suitcase to find her one sweater. *It's hard to get over my head.* She stared at her hands. *It used to be big enough to cover my arms.*

Back to the window. *"The sunlight is more slanted. But the sidewalk looks the same. No school buses. But today is Saturday."*

Back to the door of the lady from Venezuela. The lady answered this time. Gabriela motioned to use her phone. *That lady has the same Emergency button that Abuelita's phone has.*

A brusque lady answered. In English.

"Yes, there was an ambulance transfer from near this location yesterday."

"Where did they take Abuelita? My Abuelita?"

"They took a patient to the hospital nearest to this location. That is all the information I have."

"Do you know what happened to Abuelita?"

"No, I can't tell you anything about her. Call them. Or go there."

The line hummed. *That phone lady doesn't answer anymore.*

Gabriela ran back to her apartment. She grabbed her coat. *There aren't very many people outside today. Everybody seems to be in a hurry.*

The air in the hall was kind of yellow. Dusty. Gabriela wrinkled her nose and coughed.

Once.

People started staring. Fear shone in their eyes above their masks. She hunched. Put her hand to her mouth. *Abuelita says the rules for masks keep changing. That I need to be "little."*

She could hear the elevator coming. She ran. The cables groaned as the elevator halted. Its frame shook. The door creaked slowly open. *Just in time.*

Gabriela slid on and grabbed the ancient handrail with one hand. She used the other hand to punch the button marked "G."

***

Dr. Ben circled back through the ICU and peered through the window to Isabella's bed. The petite chest moved to the cycle of the ventilator. A dialysis nurse was hooking up new machines.

He adjusted his mask, gowned up, gloved up, and backed through the door. He grabbed a light from the counter. Went to the opposite side of the bed. Opened Isabella's eyelids to check her pupils. Larger on the left. Blown pupil on the left. Right, minimally reactive.

He repeated the maneuver three times. *Hemorrhagic conversion of what had appeared to be an embolic stroke. Will this never end?*

Back to the hallway. He tossed the gown and gloves into the receptacle.

He punched his phone to the operator. "This is Dr. Ben Lawson in ICU. Can you have the neurosurgeon on call please contact me as soon as he breaks scrub on the current case?"

He checked the hallway computer. Isabella was now number five on the list. He reordered the CT. This time STAT and to evaluate for hemorrhagic stroke.

Dr. Ben looked around, then kicked a trash receptacle that teamed with discarded protective gear. A few paper gowns wafted to the floor.

He didn't pick them up.

Urgency likely won't push Isabella any higher on the list today.

Twenty-six more patients to see. All nearly as sick as Isabella. *Hopefully, more straightforward than this one.*

* * *

Dr. Steinham wandered to the counter and slapped Dr. Ben on the back. "Say, want to go get a drink tonight? When we are done?"

Dr. Ben Lawson continued his note, barely flinching from the slap. "It's only early afternoon."

He keyboarded again, hit "send," and turned to Steinham. "We never get done. But we could use something different."

"Well, the equinox is this Thursday! Time to party, virus or none!"

Steinham let out a low whistle.

16

Abuelita! Where did they take my abuelita? Gabriela ran out the front door of the apartment building. *She must be at the big hospital.*

A car with an L sign in its front window waited—with the motor running, its passenger door open.

Gabriela jumped in and slammed the car door.

The driver opened his droopy eyelids above his mask and turned his neck. "You don't look like the picture on my phone." His brown eyes scanned her tiny frame. "Do you know enough numbers to check my license plate?"

"To the nearest hospital," Gabriela asserted. "That's what the phone lady said."

The driver's jaw frowned beneath his mask, but he released the brake, and the car swerved into traffic.

Gabriela placed her chin on the back of the front seat. She scanned the driver's eyes in the rear-view mirror.

"You look like my older brother. I think he's still in Mexico."

The driver pointed to a small cloth flag dangling from his rearview mirror. A green flag with a white moon and one star.

His eyes smiled in the mirror's reflection.

Gabriela shifted back in the seat. *He seems nice. But there is no red in that flag.*

The car drove many blocks, then stopped in front of a big glass building with an H on it. Gabriela pulled the handle and jumped out.

"Hey, little girl. Are you sure it's your credit card that ordered this ride?" The driver yelled after her in accented English.

"Mi abuelita me necesita," Gabriela yelled as she raced down the sidewalk toward the enormous building with the H on it.

Across the parking lot, a dark-haired person straightened in the driver's seat of a white sedan, her eyes following a little girl in a plaid skirt who ran toward the side door. Blue surgical scrubs bent to pull a white lab coat from the passenger's floor space. The metal banding of a stethoscope glinted beyond the windshield. The dark-haired driver opened the door of the sedan, slid on the white lab coat and a surgical mask, then grabbed the stethoscope from the dash and flung it around her neck. The quiet figure walked a distance behind the little girl.

Yellow tape blocked the front swinging door, but the huge shadow of a person emerged from the side door. Gabriela slid behind the shadow before the door closed. She swooshed into a large room with high ceilings.

Her eyes got big. Little walls hid beds with sick people. People in yellow gowns bustled about. The masks hid their faces.

Her lower lip trembled. *It's hard to understand what they are saying.*

Her chest got big. Tears burst down her cheeks. "Abuelita! Mi abuelita!"

The doorman rushed to grab her. "Shush, little girl." He hushed his finger to his mask. "You know you can't come in here without special permission. You should find a mask small enough to fit you."

People in the room glared. Gabriela's widened eyes looked back to the door.

Then someone patted the top of her head. "Little girl, let me see if I can help you." A huge man with a big belly and a blue uniform stood offering a tiny mask from his hand. "Who are you here to see?"

Her eyes saw the big word with the first letters, "SECurity" over his chest. *We didn't learn that word at school.*

The huge man took her firmly by the elbow. They skated on glistening waxed floors toward a glowing pink sign that said "Emer."

"I'm glad they have these letters at school," she sniffled in a tiny voice. The man kept his hand on Gabriela's elbow, but he slowed his walk. They glided through another door, where a masked lady stood on a tiny platform.

The lady looked down at Gabriela and then at the man. "Who is she? And what is she doing here?"

The big-bellied man nudged Gabriela in the lady's direction. "I don't know. She made it through the front door. She keeps saying she wants to see her grandmother. Claims her grandmother was brought here yesterday."

The lady grunted.

Gabriela stepped closer and careened her neck upward. "Her last name starts with the last letter—Z."

The lady scrolled on her computer. "Zapota? Yes, brought here yesterday. Went directly to the ICU."

"Which ICU?" asked the man, his hand still gripping Gabriela's elbow.

"Respiratory or medical ICU. One of them. They're putting them all on the same floor." The lady continued scrolling on her computer.

A dark-haired woman whisked behind them, tucking the stethoscope in the pocket of her lab coat, name tag turned inward. She punched a button for the staff elevator.

The huge man propelled Gabriela's lifted arm toward the public elevator. Gabriella looked back, concerned. "Lady, does your neck work?" *I don't think they hear me.*

The man answered his phone. He hit the button for the sixth floor. They swooshed up, and he gently pushed her out of the elevator.

Alone.

Gabriela stared at a carpeted room with enormous windows on one side. Masked people in yellow gowns were coming in and out of a door under a sign with the letters "ICU."

A dark-haired person in blue surgical scrubs arose from her chair. "Little girl, you may have to wait for a few minutes until you get to see your grandma."

She pulled something crinkly out of the white coat slung over her arm. "How about some candy while you wait?"

Gabriela took the candy and unwrapped it. *It is so pretty.*

She popped it in her mouth beneath her new mask. *It is so yummy. I'll just hold it in my mouth for a while.*

She scrunched her coat onto the seat next to the lady and yawned.

17

This virus will make you a child again—vulnerable, dependent, afraid—others telling you lies or truths, others deciding for you. Out of control.

18

It took a small army to get Isabella to the CT scanner. The dialysis nurse needed to interrupt her renal therapy; respiratory therapy needed to manage her airway as her ventilator was wrapped and moved; pharmacists needed to verify all medications, including those interrupted. Her IVs were wrapped; they might have to be changed. Qualified nursing personnel needed to accompany the patient. All personnel had to have shoe covers, gowns, masks, and gloves to even touch her bed. It took some three hours just to get her there.

The neurosurgeon found Dr. Ben waiting outside the CT scanner. He had already reviewed the CT of her head. "Large hemorrhage compressing the brain stem. Usually, the blood pressure is high, not low, in these cases. There must be a confounding factor." He paused.

Dr. Ben offered no explanation.

The neurosurgeon turned to leave. "But if she has a chance to live, I need to evacuate that clot as soon as possible. If you can get a consent signed for the operating room, I'll squeeze her in as the next case."

"Well, she has no family other than a five- or six-year-old granddaughter, who isn't here," Dr. Ben argued. "The granddaughter can't legally sign for her, anyhow."

The neurosurgeon adjusted his mask over the bags below his eyes. He turned to walk away, mumbling something about a Good Samaritan clause. "I think this will have to be a case of implied consent."

* * *

The sun began to hide behind the trees. Afternoon coolness settled in the hallway. The panic of adrenaline faded into fatigue, dread descending as the minutes lagged.

Dr. Ben interrupted ICU visits to check on Isabella on a stretcher in the hall. *The monitor shows her blood pressure is now 100/diastolic. Maybe the dopamine is helping. Or is it that her CRRT is interrupted? Her oxygenation is better with the ventilator and the additional proning.*

But how can anesthesia position her for surgery? Well, the anesthesiologist will know soon—at least for this patient. So much for a randomized controlled clinical trial.

He added a nebulizer treatment "on call to surgery" to the pre-op orders. *Unclear if this will help, but I want to give her every chance to survive.*

Four p.m. finally arrived. The respiratory therapist gave Isabella the nebulizer treatment. Masked and gowned staff wheeled her stretcher to the OR.

Dr. Ben took a deep breath. *At least someone else is in charge of her care during surgery.*

His phone buzzed twice. The first text urged, "Low blood pressure, room 10, ICU." The second: "Newly intubated patient, room 14, ICU. Need orders."

19

Isabella returned from the operating room within ninety minutes. The huge white bandage on her head made her face appear even darker.

The neurosurgeon found Dr. Ben in the ICU. "There is something bizarre about these patients. When I removed her clot, she immediately formed another clot in its place. She's on a heparin drip, for God's sake! This shouldn't be happening!"

"The other physicians report it's happening repeatedly. Regardless of which anticoagulant we use."

"Is there another pathway for clots to form? Besides the two we learned in medical school?"

"Maybe this new virus acts like a poison? Maybe it's so toxic that it triggers huge amounts of inflammation and clot?"

"It's as if everything we learned isn't working. Every patient we touch dies. Of course, they might die sooner without us, but this is crazy!" The neurosurgeon held up a gloved hand. "Well, you internists figure it out. I'm going back to the operating room."

"If they died without us, at least it would be cheaper!" Dr. Ben dropped his eyes.

Dr. Fadheel whisked in from the tent and stood under the furnace vent to warm his hands. "What about all these people who have a positive test but never even get sick, never get low oxygen, and never get clots?"

"But if the patient gets sick at all, he or she can decompensate quickly," Dr. Cohen, pulmonologist, cautioned from his mask, through his steamed eyeglasses. "And they die alone."

He stood to face Dr. Fadheel. "And fast. They're texting on their phone in ICU, granted with an oxygen level of 40% instead of the 95% they should have. But they're still alert. And six hours later, they're dead."

"I overheard a nurse who's worked in ICU for forty years say she's never seen anything like this," Dr. Santos inserted from his computer station. "And even she can't tell who's going to die and who's going to get out of here alive."

Dr. Fadheel walked over to the counter. "The newscasters say it's the old, the hypertensives, the men—but I saw a 41-year-old daughter in the tent two days ago. She brought her 79-year-old dad with chronic lung and heart disease. They both had positive tests. He went home the same day she died. Who will we include in the clinical trials?"

Dr. Santos cleared his throat. Beneath his mask, of course. "If we can ever stop the dying long enough to think about criteria for a clinical trial."

"There has to be more to this than what we know." Dr. Cohen stopped short of the door. "We need one affordable blood test to risk-stratify patients—to know whom to keep in the ICU, whom to place in the step-down unit, and whom to allow home. Seems practical and cost-saving to me."

Dr. Clarke sat quietly, ear pods bulging in the front pocket beneath his yellow gown. As usual, he just sat, looked at x-rays, and typed notes.

Finally, he stood, fumbling his stethoscope beneath the yellow surgical gown to the pocket of his white lab coat. "We don't know how to treat them. Our drugs are not working. And we can't even advise the patients in person—or discuss with their families by phone—how to plan. It's like we're dancing on a moving carpet."

He looked at Dr. Ben. A wizardly knowing passed his eyes above the mask.

"Makes you wonder why you worked your bloody ass off to get through all this training—no more difference than it seems to make!"

20

Dr. Steinham flexed his legs on the magazine table in the doctors' lounge. He thumbed his phone. "Where are you, anyhow?"

Dr. Ben reviewed Isabella's orders. One more time. Then forwarded his sign-out to the night doctor.

* * *

Steinham's BMW headed to a sketchy part of town. "Say, where are we going?" Ben stared at the cityscape whirling by the passenger window. "I skipped dinner thinking I could eat at the club."

"Oh, I know a club with great dancers. Their hamburgers are decent." Steinham steered his BMW through the empty streets. "We need a break." The neon sign ahead advertised exotic dancers.

Suddenly Ben was inside. The stale dark was oppressive. A spotlight on the stage highlighted girls twirling, writhing around their poles. The sound of skin scraping metal added to the scratching of the boombox. *I haven't been in such a place since I was a sophomore in college. Once was enough, and I don't think I need this tonight either.*

However, Steinham was downing his third beer, tipping the dancers, and swinging his hips to the music.

Ben finished his hamburger and nursed the first half of his second beer. *Three more hours.*

A dancer headed his way, this time in a red and black gown with generous cleavage and a slit revealing extensive thigh. She was very white with blue-streaked auburn hair, heavy makeup. He strained to see a recognizable person beneath the lipstick and eyelashes.

She stroked his back with her long nails. *Keep that up. Feels good. Had forgotten.* She sat, her thighs opened on his lap, her lips meeting his. *Had forgotten this too.* A few deepening nips, then the throat. She had a very long and effective tongue.

She is somebody's daughter. Maybe somebody's sister.

Ben blushed and stiffened. He slid his feet beneath the table.

The dancer quit Ben's lap and headed next to Steinham, who eagerly accepted her invitation to dance. Steinham started to the back with her when he stumbled.

She pushed Steinham into the nearest chair. At a table far from the counter. "Guess you need to come here more often," the dancer teased.

I think five beers have hit their mark.

Ben glanced across the lounge. A brunette huddled over a small circular table, her sequined bottom pointing to the stage.

"Six years old, huh?" The seated man with a two-day beard looked hopeful. "A virgin?"

"Yep, pretty certain. Think about it," the brunette quipped. She flipped her purple fingernails to the man.

"Is she white?"

"No, brown. But light brown."

The man frowned.

"You need some entertainment while you think it over." The brunette led him offside through a curtained doorway.

Ben noticed eyes peering between the curtains to the left of the stage. The eyes looked familiar. They were young. Innocent. Afraid.

He had seen these eyes before. His head fuzzed. They seemed to watch him from a lower height. Like an animal or a child?

He felt sweat drip under his shirt. He looked around the club. *What am I doing in this place?* The stage, the dancers, the men hovering like monsters surveying prey.

Ben stood, slapped Steinham on the back, and bellowed, "Well, Steinham, time to hit the road. Tomorrow comes early."

Steinham did not resist. Ben herded him to the door. They were just outside when a blinding light, with the crackle of gravel, lit up the parking lot. Ben took no notice. He had the keys and a firm grip on Steinham's shoulder. He lurched Steinham into the front passenger's seat and slammed the door. He fumbled with the ignition on the BMW, then headed for the freeway.

I hope my memories from the year-end party last spring will help me tonight.

Ben sped up to blend with the traffic heading to the suburb where Steinham lived.

Steinham usually lives alone, and I don't recall him bragging about any recent girlfriend moving in.

The windows to Steinham's apartment were dark. Ben threw the BMW keys to Steinham, who stood in the driveway.

He walked to his own car and kicked the gravel off his shoes as he got behind the wheel. Back to the hotel. *Another day, tomorrow.*

21

Maia finished the dancing, the pole. No further customers. She opened her envelope in the hall backstage. *Cash. Accurate. As promised.*

A small girl, about five or six, turned from the curtains behind the stage and ventured into Maia's dressing room. Maia followed her.

Maia's snack—a plastic bag with a sandwich and an orange—still lay on the makeup table.

"What are you doing here?"

The child eyed the sandwich. She adjusted her coat on her arm.

"Where are you from, little girl?"

"I'm from Mexico. My abuelita is at the big hospital. That lady with the brown hair brought me here." The child peered at the orange. "She said she would take me home tonight when she's done with work."

"And where is home?"

"The apartments where we live."

"And where is that?"

"I don't know," Gabriela stammered.

"And what did you say your name is?" Maia asked.

"My name is Ga-brie-la." The child turned from the sandwich in disgust. "If you want to call me that. Instead of 'little girl.'"

"Okay, Ga-brie-la. Did I say that correctly? Gabriela."

The child nodded, eyes darting back to the sandwich.

"By the way, Gabriela, you can have my sandwich. And my orange."

The little girl tore open the plastic bag and gulped the bread and cheese. She polished the orange as if it were a rare treasure and slowly put it in her coat pocket.

Maia moved her head to see beyond the part in the curtain. Across the lounge, the brunette was talking to a male customer. *Looks like she might be a while.*

"Gabriela, let's see if you can tell me where you live."

"It's not very far."

"The nearest bus stop is eight blocks away. Can you walk that far?"

Their shoes left footprints in the gravel edging the street. When they joined the sidewalk, Maia grasped Gabriela's hand. The streetlights soon glistened on the head of the child, almost dancing, bopping along beside Maia.

Where am I going to go with this kid? Just a little younger than my niece? Maybe she needs help.

It was warmer on the bus. Sitting below the heating vent, Gabriela nodded. Her eyes closed. Her head drooped on Maia's shoulder. Soon, a soft snoring.

The gaping eyes of several apartment complexes passed beyond the reflections of the windows. *I wonder if any of these are where this kid belongs?*

The driver roared out the next stop. Maia abrupted her doze, shook her head, and adjusted her mask. She nudged Gabriela.

"Hey, little girl, is this where you get off?"

"Yes," nodded Gabriela.

Gabriela stood and lock-stepped Maia like a younger sister. Off the bus, standing with stiff knees on the sidewalk, shafts of moonlight dodging the clouds.

Maia knelt to see the face. "Where did you say you live?"

The little girl shivered. "I don't know, but I don't think it's here."

Maia took a deep breath. *What do I do with this kid? Is it even legal to be taking her with me? Is this truly better than leaving her with the brunette who brought her to the club?*

She took Gabriela's hand and started toward her house-apartment. "We'll find who you belong to tomorrow."

* * *

In the morning, Gabriela met Chloe the cat, sleeping at the foot of her couch.

She played with Chloe all of the next day. Even arranged the blankets for her new friend.

As she petted Chloe, her forehead wrinkled. *Is Abuelita still at the big hospital?*

She didn't ask.

She ate only enough to keep the cramps out of her stomach.

I need to smile.

All the time.

22

Ben slept like a drugged man. His phone dinged at 6:40 a.m. He bowled across the room, his bare feet dancing in the cold.

He glimpsed the caller ID.

Laura. Ben let out a long breath. His eyes turned upward.

"Did you see the newspaper today?"

"No, I just got up," Ben managed. "Haven't had time."

"Well, Steinham finally made the front page," Laura smoldered. "The guy behind him looks suspiciously like Yours Truly!"

"I have no idea what you're talking about." Ben climbed underneath the still warm blankets.

"Well, the headline says that COVID is causing accelerated burnout in physicians. Apparently, one of their photographers grabbed a picture of two doctors exiting a club. One looks very much like you. Were you there?"

"I went there with Steinham for a hamburger and a beer. I had no idea where he wanted to go. I swear

I didn't touch a lady, didn't tip a dancer. I had two beers, was perfectly sober, and got him out of there before he disgraced us."

"Well, he may not be disgraced, but I am! I would have thought he had enough medical credentials to make the journals without going to the public domain."

"I'm sorry, I'm truly sorry. I had no intention of hurting you or our relationship."

"Well, you can be as sorry as you want to be, but I'm calling my attorney Monday morning as soon as the office is open."

"Laura, Laura." Ben spoke gently. "I swear I did nothing to upset you. I simply went with Steinham to get a beer. I had two," Ben repeated. "He had more, but I got him out of there before he made a disgrace of himself or our profession."

"I thought your only mistress was medicine. How dare you spend hours in a club in a sketchy part of the city? God knows what you did while you were there!"

Ben smiled. Laura's anger made her cute. He liked her energy. *Better than her depression.*

"God knows I did nothing to disgrace you, me, or our relationship. I went there simply to get a beer. I did not choose the place, and I did nothing with any women. I didn't even tip a dancer. I had two beers, and I got Steinham out of there."

"I can't believe you would threaten our relationship this way! I'm out of town with three kids, trying to make school work remotely, trying to act as if this is a vacation—and you, and you! You make the newspaper patronizing a club with exotic dancers! Do you have any idea what my parents will think? What our friends will think?"

"I told you I'm terribly sorry. I only went there to help a friend—I had two beers, and I got him out of there."

"And what do you think your medical colleagues will say?"

"What the newspaper says." Ben tightened his jaw. "That we're all burned out and that we need a break."

"Yeah, well, what about the rest of your family? Don't you think we need a break? I'm burned out too! Burned out with remote school taking only a quarter of the usual time, back with my parents and their stinking rules, trying to keep three kids corralled. And I'm not going to any club!"

"I'm so sorry."

"Well, not as sorry as you're going to be when you hear from my attorney—and my dad!"

Dial tone. *It isn't like Laura to hang up. She must have accidentally hit the mute button.*

Ben dragged himself out of the bed and left the sheets in a heap. The mirror above the sink highlighted the bags under his eyes. He plunged his face into the cold water.

He sprinted about the room, trying to find his clothes. "No, not those." He pitched yesterday's pants and shirt onto the floor.

In the far end of the closet, he found fresh clothes, back from the dry cleaner's delivery, including a clean white lab coat. He pulled his newest shoes from the closet floor.

Mother would be proud. Today is Sunday.

* * *

Today is Sunday. Taxis will be slow. The subway is diminished to two lines. But I can drive. Parking is an option today.

Ben's scowling face scanned the rearview mirror. "Laura can't be serious." He sat up taller.

He chewed his lip. Had his six-year-old son heard Laura's tirade this morning? Would his son believe he was really trying to help a friend? Or would he think his dad was a louse and a womanizer? And never around? Worse yet, that his dad had time for other women but no time for his son? And that was just the son—never mind the five-year-old and eight-year-old daughters.

The drive to the hospital was quick; there was no traffic and the usually teeming parking lot was nearly empty. He parked, badged in, and went to the doctors' lounge. There were bagels, a toaster, and fresh coffee in the lounge. He had ten minutes to sit before sign-in rounds.

He had just sat down when his phone buzzed. Steinham texted he would be there about 10 a.m. Could Ben cover his patients until he got there?

23

A whispering came into the doctors' lounge. It whispered that Dr. Clapham wasn't coming in today. It was quietly repeated, person to person, that he wouldn't be coming in again *ever*. No, he hadn't died of COVID. He had taken a gun to himself.

Apparently, his wife and five-year-old daughter found him.

Dr. Ben took a deep breath.

The whispers designated who would take the patients who were to have been seen by Dr. Clapham. Nurses had moist eyes and sniffles. Doctors spoke quietly and minimally. Nothing was said about Dr. Clapham. *Saving their energy in order to take care of the extra patients*?

Each introduced himself or herself to Dr. Clapham's patients as if he were at the beach—simply, "I'll be seeing you today on behalf of your usual physician."

None of the patients—even those not sedated, not on the ventilator—questioned the change of personnel.

24

Jakeem squinted. *If only this headache would go away.* Lots of new patient admissions the last two weeks from the hospital—all having had COVID, and all having been weaned from ventilators. They were as weak as cats, unable to take care of themselves. Worse, some of their living places had closed while they were in the hospital. Others claimed they weren't wanted back.

They were still hoarse. *Must be caused by being weaned off the ventilator? But is the COVID still hanging around?*

Some claimed their loved ones couldn't see them, even though their loved ones were at home, either having lost their jobs or having been furloughed. The relatives could come by and wave through the windows.

Some drove by. Nobody honked. *It would draw attention?*

One lady celebrated her anniversary, and her hubby came up to the window and blew kisses. He showed her flowers he had bought for her, even though she couldn't receive them.

Masks were getting in short supply. And all that "gowning and dressing" was slipping away.

People started to miss work, and they didn't bother to call in. They said they were afraid of the virus. They couldn't afford to miss work, but they really couldn't afford to die! Their folks needed them.

Jakeem decided he could take their shifts. *A chance to get ahead. More money for Granny, more money for me.*

Jakeem scurried through the patients' long lists of therapies and their longer lists of medications. On Monday, he paid no mind to his sore throat. He couldn't smell real good—in fact, he started toileting patients by the clock instead of the nose. On Thursday, he got the diarrhea himself—*a real nuisance when trying to take care of thirteen residents.* He started coughing. *My TB test is negative. Nothing to worry about.*

The announcer on the TV in a patient's room said obesity was a risk factor for the virus. *I should watch my diet, but I am a BIG boy and entitled to eat my share—especially when I'm working this hard.*

On Friday, he was tired. *Bone tired.* He checked his blood pressure at work: 165/95. *Not bad. But it is above the recommended 130/80. These long days must be catching up with me.*

Yesterday, Saturday, he was short of breath. *Must be the rainy weather. Or smog from the city?*

This morning, Momma said it was time to go to Sunday meetin'.

Not going. I'm really tired. I can't dance or even sing when I'm this short of breath.

And his legs were swelling. *Now, this is new.* His sac was swelling. *This is really not normal.*

Jakeem made it to the tent outside the hospital by early Sunday afternoon. *I have to get better before work on Monday night.*

Jakeem didn't make it past the screening. His rapid PCR test was positive for the coronavirus and his pulse oximetry was 91%. He was sent directly to the hospital and triaged to the observation area. *Nobody seems worried about my swelling.*

His head throbbed. They said his pulse oximetry was now 88%. They hooked five liters of oxygen by a cannula in his nose. An hour later, they increased this to ten liters of oxygen.

By midafternoon, his headache was horrible. *My head, my head! Icepicks in my brain*! The nurse told him his oxygen level had dropped again. "We're moving you to the ICU."

He touched his cell phone to call Granny.

Granny picked up on the fifth ring.

"Hey, Granny," he started. "I be at the hospital."

He could hear the clatter of plates in her cupboard. Somebody rapping at her door. Yelling.

"They think I have the virus that's been causin' crib. I feel lousy. I called to say, 'I love you.'"

A dog barked in the background. More yelling.

"I'll let you know when I get out."

Buzz. *Granny must have dropped the phone.*

"You know," he turned to the nurse, "it's lonely in here. I'm used to being around lots of people. They say I'm a people person."

The nurse raised an eyebrow, nodded understanding, and replaced the oxygen cannula with an oxygen mask. "There, there, you can relax now. No talking, please."

"This. Well, THIS. This is not gonna make it!"

"Talking uses up your oxygen," the nurse clarified.

He thought of his women. Even the ones who had broken up with him. *I wonder if they know I'm in the hospital. Can they even come and see me? Their comin', though, might make this better.* Well, the one who busted his ribs and bruised his liver with the chair—that one best stay away.

Dr. Ben Lawson came into his room, garbed like an alien. He was all business.

"Mr. Robert," Dr. Lawson started, "this may not surprise you, but you are very sick. So sick, in fact, that we may have to put a breathing tube down your windpipe to keep the oxygen in your blood high enough. That should help your headache. Before you get too sleepy, I would like you to read these papers and think about signing them."

Jakeem looked at the papers. He could read part of the words. They said something about them putting a breathing tube down. *Sounds awful. But if it comes to that, that's what I'll have to do.*

Granny said you shouldn't trust white man's medicine, that it might bring you a fast endin' without you even knowin' it.

But right now, I feel horrible. Anything to help this headache. He signed the papers.

He picked up his phone and sent a text message to his work and one to Cherika, the last girlfriend he really cared about. *Maybe her newest guy has left her. Maybe she'll think about me after all.*

The room became eerily quiet. Some five medical-type people including Dr. Lawson, dressed like yellow canaries, came into the room. They mumbled that there was a shortage of some medicines, that his oxygen was dangerously low. He felt a twinge of pain in his IV arm, then the world started swirling. His muscles got weaker. *I think I'm going to go to sleep and sleep forever.* In fact, he wasn't certain, but *maybe the Heaven that Momma talked about was right up there in that ceiling.*

He came up in the warm black cloud. Suddenly, he was hovering. He was flying like an airplane. But he was a little boy. His body was only about four feet long. That day on the playground. He was trying to catch the ball. Suddenly, the batter hit him square in the jaw. He lost his balance and fell slow-like onto the sidewalk. His head felt like it splintered. Blackness. Yelling. Dark shadows over him. The black haze seemed to last a long time. When he next could see, Granny and his mom were hovering over him.

"Hey, Granny," he thought to say. "How 'bout singing one of those songs like they do at your church? My songs may not be the best here. They be misunderstood."

The tune of a song danced about in his head, teasing and twisting like a kite on a breezy day. He tried to catch it. It made him want to dance. But then, he was too tired to get his feet moving. Seems like he should be groovin' to this tune, but what tune was it? Was he beatin' right?

Suddenly he was fishing with his brother, the cool wind hitting his jacket, and the pole trailing in the wind. He felt a tug on the end of the line. He jumped in excitement. This one was going to be a big one for a real nice meal. The fish leaped into the air and became a dragon that was breathing fire in his throat. The dragon was winning. This fire hurt like hell! He felt a huge pipe scrape the inside of his nose and go down where the dragon was firing. He hoped it was a hose with some water.

His head felt big and swollen. *He floated where he couldn't control his body or where his kite would fly. He twisted.* Sudden, horrible nausea. He twisted again and stared into the tiles on the floor. Suddenly he was looking into the light in the ceiling. There were ants crawling about the cracks up there. *Don't they know enough to spray this place? This is a hospital, after all!*

Huge cockroaches, attached to those clear tubes, ran up his arms. He tried to swat them. But strong bands tied his hands down. *Some really mean dude made my life crib—to have bugs close enough to bite you but not be able to kill them. I'll punch this guy, or worse, when I get out of here.*

A piece of sweet potato pie floated by his mouth. That'll taste really good, if I can just get the right angle to have a bite. Oh, but pie could attract more bugs.

Sure looked good, though.

He got to decide whether to be happy, whether to sleep. It didn't seem to matter. He floated above the bed. Or in the bed? *Not sure which.*

A runny white frosting started up that clear tube into his arm. He felt sleepy, his eyes heavy. The pain in his throat faded. *He floated softly. This time, in the bed.*

The EKG continued to march across the screen above his head. The ventilator cycled to breathe for him. Jakeem's CNA classes hadn't discussed a medically induced coma.

* * *

Dr. Ben Lawson spent four hours trying to stabilize Jakeem, making multiple adjustments in the ventilator settings and rehearsing options with the renal consultant. And answering phone calls, several from a woman named Cherika. Cherika insisted that her daughter with Mr. Robert was now thirteen and needed a father in her life, so Dr. Ben best keep him alive. But Cherika was not listed in the computer as the patient's next-of-kin nor was she on the list of HIPAA-approved contacts. *Listen. Be professional but kind.*

And Jakeem Robert was only one of Dr. Ben Lawson's patients.

Buzz: Priority text from the CMO. *We have reduced supplies of PPE. Use them only for intubations in ICU, as these represent the highest risk for catching this virus. More supplies should arrive this week.*

Buzz: Text from the compliance officer. *This daughter wants to speak with a doctor, not a nurse, about her father.*

Call: "Yes, I understand he was the CEO of an investment company. Yes, he is very sick. However, we have many sick patients, and we need your help."

Listen.

"No, you cannot come here. The hospital is in quarantine, and the closest you can get is the hospital parking lot. Yes, some subways have reduced service."

Listen. Then try to explain.

"Yes, I know your father is an important man. However, the hospital rules apply to everyone."

Listen. Stay awake, alert.

"However, could you please emphasize that staying on his stomach will help his oxygen level?"

Listen. Be kind and professional.

"Yes, I know he hasn't rested on his tummy since he was three years old."

Listen. Try to convey understanding.

"I understand he thinks the doctors and nurses don't know what they're doing, but this is important. We don't want to sedate him and put a breathing tube down his throat to breathe for him unless we have no other options."

Listen. Shuffle your feet to stay awake. Tonight, you'll get to sleep.

"Yes, I know he might forget this within two minutes of your talking with him, but thank you for trying to help."

Listen.

"Yes, thank you for calling. It's always a pleasure to speak with you."

He punched the red button. *A pleasure?*

* * *

Dr. Charlie Lee rustled beside Dr. Ben's shoulder. "Are you still here? I thought you made it home three days ago."

"Well, I didn't make it home. But I did get some sleep. At the hotel." Ben looked up from his computer screen. "You look like a zombie—the mask with the gown, gloves, and shoe covers."

"Well, maybe I *have* become a zombie. I'm still thinking it must be morning." Dr. Charlie chuckled, then paused. "I just visited a lady in ICU, and her bedside monitor said it was 5:25 p.m."

"Yes, Charlie, sometimes it's hard to tell if it's day or night. But today is a Sunday. And it's evening. About the middle of March. We usually don't get text messages from the CEO on weekends, especially on

Sundays. But they're here too. Fixated or guilted? Who knows?"

"That lady in room 14 looks like she might pass. Her family has been calling."

"Too bad they can't come and be with her."

New inputs lighted the computer screen. Dr. Ben brightened. "Ah, Mr. Robert's lab is back. His ferritin, CRP, CPK, and d-dimer are high, his platelets and lymphocytes low."

"Who knows what those labs mean with this virus?"

"Well, these labs suggest things are headed in the wrong direction."

Dr. Ben studied the screen outside Jakeem's ICU room. *The oxygen measurement is improved on the ventilator.* He peered through the side window. Jakeem looked strong, even strapped to a bed.

Who knows if Jakeem will get the inflammatory cascade that makes these people clot until they die? Who knows if he'll make it out of this place alive or join the frozen bodies in one of the trucks behind the hospital?

* * *

Dr. Charlie peeked over Ben's shoulder at his computer screen. "I'm likely violating HIPAA, but your patient's risk profile is even more worrisome than his labs. He's a thirty-eight-year-old African American male, with a BMI of 32. And a blood pressure of 150/93."

"The computer doesn't list if he has type A or O blood. And his vitamin D level isn't back yet."

"Well, his glucose isn't elevated."

"But he is obese, and he has hypertension. I'm concerned he has latent diabetes or at least insulin resistance."

Charlie plunked on the rolling stool next to the counter. "Do you ever wonder if there's some factor we're missing? Why is your guy so sick and others have a positive test and they feel just fine? Or they think they just have a mild cold."

"Well, it's a qualitative, not a truly quantitative test, with a fairly high false negative rate."

"Before this, they said you had to have a high positive predictive value and a low rate of false negatives. Using a test with a high false negative rate makes it hard to limit a pandemic."

"This is the best we have. Somehow, we need two things—a reliable first test to see who is infected and, if infected, a better test to predict who will get really sick or even die from this virus." Dr. Ben sighed. "For now, retesting for infection—a few days later—is all we have."

"You always got a higher grade in epidemiology than I did."

"Well, it never made a difference until now."

Dr. Charlie pulled his stool closer to Dr. Ben and sat down. "Do you ever wish, Ben, that we were back in college, where you could think something and pretend it's true? Where thoughts made reality, or at least increased the probability that something could be true?"

"Yeah, all the time."

"We had all the answers then." Charlie downed the last dregs of cold coffee and crunched the foam cup.

"Well, we were young. Maybe naïve. We sure don't have all the answers now." Dr. Ben moved his clipboard to the next counter. "As I say, we need a test with a better predictive value. Maybe someday, we'll have one."

Dr. Charlie stood to untwist his back. "Well, Dr. Jones is using a different protocol and seeing fewer deaths."

"Dr. Jones is no longer with us. Seems his protocol got him in trouble here. Rumor says he's at a different hospital across town."

"Yeah, he's a bit of a maverick. Thinks for himself. Not the type to wait for randomized controlled trials."

Dr. Ben massaged the mouse for his computer. "Do we have the time, likely two years, needed for randomized studies? Is it even ethical to have a control group with this virus? Who wants to be in the control group for this virus?"

"Not me." Dr. Charlie winced. "Give me every chance to survive."

"Maybe observational studies are the best we have right now. With a new virus, who knows what will work?"

"Hindsight is 20/20. Guess we'll know someday. Probably after we finish here."

"If we don't catch this virus and die first." Dr. Ben pressed his lips together.

"Well, at least the public will think we're heroes." Dr. Charlie hit the trash can on his first try. He headed for the door.

Positive thoughts, Ben. Positive thoughts.

By the way, the patient's notes on your computer are still not signed.

25

Dr. Ben made it home Sunday evening. The computer at work and his phone said it was March 15, 2020.

Laura had called with her rant that morning. From Florida. *Unlikely to infect my family with this virus now.*

He was tired of the hotel, the hospital, the cold meals, and coffee in disposable cups. *A shower in my own bathroom and sleeping in my own bed might help.*

He entered through the garage, dust and stale air greeting him. No dog.

He shivered. The thermostat was set at 65 degrees.

A rap on the front door. The neighbor had seen Ben's car pull into the driveway, so he was bringing the dog home, along with the bag of dog food, the dog's dish and water container. And the dog's brush.

He was also delivering a box of mail. "Your mailbox is drowning. Check for bills."

Ben thanked the man and took the dog's leash.

He posted the dog in the hallway and headed for the kitchen. He threw the mail onto the counter, just missing an open peanut butter jar and a half-open loaf of bread molding in its plastic bag.

Ben opened the refrigerator door. Sour milk, wilted vegetables. A few eggs, uncracked, lining the bottom of a carton.

He staggered to the kitchen table and lifted a newspaper dated March 2, 2020. A pencil landed on the floor. The Arts section showcased a half-done crossword puzzle.

His eyes landed on the kids' backpacks from school, along with their boots, hats, and mittens scattered in the entrance. *That's right. They're in Florida.*

He checked the laundry room and opened the washing machine. Smelly, mildewed towels, half dry. *They must have left in a hurry.*

He banged on the washing machine lid. *How is this craziness affecting all of us, not just the kids?*

His marriage—well, it had started out so hopefully, only to be squashed by long hours, mounting bills, and a lonely spouse angry in her disappointment.

My in-laws have no clue how hard this is. I didn't understand how difficult this would be, or I never would have married Laura. She's correct to be angry.

He found the strongest detergent in the cupboard and slammed the door. He punched the buttons on the laundry machine. *I'll start earning a living wage about age thirty-three, some eleven years after most of my college friends and beyond the magical age of twenty-nine when most people learn they're mortal and corporate America considers you middle-aged, a risky hire.*

The mortgage on the car, the house, and the endless educational loans, together with the cost of three kids. Too much. *I'm too tired to get a moonlighting job. The cost of childcare for the kids makes Laura's working a financial draw.*

"She was correct to leave, even now." *I should never have asked her to marry me, when eighty hours of work per week is some "ideal" limit and she'll get a quarter of a spouse and her kids get a quarter of a dad.*

His phone dinged. He looked out the window. *They likely want me back at the hospital. I don't want to even know. If I don't look, I won't have to live with a guilty conscience.*

It was the ICU. Isabella had taken a turn for the worse. Her blood pressure had dropped again. She was still on dopamine. They had stopped the CRRT (renal therapy), hoping that would normalize her low blood pressure. Her EKG showed new changes consistent with a large anterior MI (heart attack). Could they still try Levophed? Yes, she was already on heparin drip and protocols indicate TPA is risky or contraindicated.

This is organ system number four going the wrong way, the lungs dependent upon a ventilator, the kidneys in failure, the brain with the strokes and the unpredictable clotting, and now the heart.

Suddenly the APACHE II score seemed a cold calculation, detached from the beautiful lady he knew was dying—unaware of her surroundings, not able to sacrifice any more for the granddaughter she had brought with her to this country.

Dr. Ben corralled the dog in its pen, grabbed a soda from the refrigerator, and headed for his car. He drove in silence. No radio, no music.

He thought of the girl child who had been with Isabella and wondered where she was. *Somewhere in this emptied city.*

"Somewhere," he parroted the paramedic and nurse who brought Isabella through the emergency room. "Somewhere. Not knowing that her grandma will never be home again."

Dr. Ben Lawson blinked to see the street. *Never home again—let alone "before the big clock outside strikes midnight."*

26

Maia stretched to remember Saturday night. Yes, cash in her purse. Slept on Sunday.

It's Monday morning, March 16. I need a run. When they're open, I'll call social services.

Two miles.

The sun is coming up. *Must be after 8 a.m.*

She jogged in place, punching her phone for the city's social services. A recording answered and left an actionless message. She held her phone against the morning light to add their phone number to her list of contacts. Called again. Left a message.

That kid must be between five and seven years old.

Maia could remember that age: *Mom and Dad were a happy couple, or so everyone thought. Shelby was a typical older sister, busy with school, her friends, church activities, and endless nighttime phone calls. She rarely slept. She was aloof, an important six years older.*

Maia was a kid.

In the way.

Maia attended ballet, soccer, spelling club, and kids' choir at church. Dana was three years old, with blonde hair, blue eyes, and a laugh that turned heads. They had family dinners, went to church, had lots of friends for playdates, had huge Christmas feasts, riotously fun vacations complete with fanciful mice and roller coaster rides, tons of hikes, visits to zoos and museums. This kid must be about the same age. What is life like for her?

Four miles done. She took a deep breath of morning air.

Maybe I'm overthinking this. Life for this kid can't be that hard.

Her cell phone pinged from her pocket. Social services calling.

This time, a real person. The lady was pleasant, took down the information, and seemed to actually care about "Gabriela, without a last name."

Lots of questions, though.

"And where did you find her? And when did you find her? Does she have any papers? Do you know where she was born? How long has she been here? Did she pass through any other countries to get here?"

"Sorry to be panting. I'm jogging this morning."

Two runners passed, motioning to Maia to pull her mask over her mouth and her nose.

"I tend bar at this establishment." Maia placed her phone between her shoulder and her mask. "This child ran through the door, yelling something in Spanish. I brought her home because she was still there when the club closed. She seemed hungry and needed a place to stay. This was late Saturday night. I figured I should call you early Monday."

The lady seemed satisfied. She said she'd start a file and call back. She actually thanked Maia for calling.

Maia zipped her phone into her jogging pants and restarted her pace.

Up this incline, hit the plateau in front of the Quik Mart. Run circles in front of the newspaper bin. Scan the headlines. More bad news about the virus, more stores and restaurants closing.

Maia smiled. *Where I work is always essential. And if I can get that job in delivery, I'll have more than enough money.*

She didn't have to worry about Tanya, the baby, the rent, or that little girl from the club.

I need to listen only to myself. My body. My choices.

Just three more miles to go.

* * *

Dr. Ben rubbed his eyes and scrolled through his computer inbox. Isabella's death certificate sprang into the queue for completion. *She must have died during the night.*

He logged onto the site:

Name: Isabella Zapota. Date of birth: Unknown. Place of birth: Mexico. Date of Death: Autofill.

Time of death: 2:50 a.m.

CAUSE OF DEATH:

1) Multiorgan failure due to

2) COVID-19 by clinical presentation and confirmed by PCR testing

He let out a breath, inserted his electronic signature, and hit *send.*

His shoulders relaxed. He exhaled deeply. *To finish something.* Numb to this resignation, this face of death.

Suddenly, eyes glared at him from the computer screen.

He stopped scrolling. *That girl child who had been with Isabella.* His brain calculated a horrible likelihood.

His eyes landed on Dr. Lee in the near-empty doctors' lounge. "Charlie, what time does the social worker get here?"

"Social workers take consults after 9 a.m.," Charlie answered. "I don't know if they have updated schedules with the pandemic, though." He pitched his cup of coffee into the trash and picked up his stethoscope.

27

Maia got the first of many calls from children's services. She learned that Gabriela's grandmother died early this morning. There is no one to claim the body, no one to organize a funeral or a memorial service. The city is deciding about mass graves for unidentified persons.

And she learned that a social worker could come tomorrow to get Gabriela. There is a foster care opening for her in a different borough of the city.

"Little girl," Maia knelt to eye level. "Gabriela." She paused. "We need to talk."

"I'm happy here," Gabriela implored. "And I can help you a whole bunch."

"Well, I like you too, but you don't belong to me. Your grandmother went to Heaven, and you'll be going to a new home soon."

I don't believe in Heaven, let alone Hell. But telling this kid that her grandmother has died and that she's going to foster care is too much.

Gabriela looked at the door, tears in her eyes.

"A nice lady will come to get you tomorrow."

Gabriela took a deep breath and stretched to be as tall as possible. "And what if I want to stay here?"

"Well, you might not have much choice. I'm sure your new home will be nice, likely a lot nicer than this apartment." Maia scanned the room. "And you can go to school, just like your grandmother wanted."

Gabriela said nothing. Her face lost its expression. Its fear.

Stony features of distrust and resolve came and stayed.

28

Gabriela listened from her bed on the living room couch. Her eyes roamed the ceiling, her feet warmed by Chloe. She lifted her head and smiled at the heavy, pokey-boney lump of cat.

Someone opened and closed the refrigerator door. Then the garage door groaned open. A car motor started. Tires reversed onto the street. *She said last night she was going to get milk and orange juice this morning.*

The garage door creaked closed.

The motor trailed into the distance.

Quiet.

Now snoring. From the direction of Tanya's bedroom.

Gabriela tiptoed to the refrigerator in the gray darkness. She grabbed some bread and lunchmeat and shoved it in a brown paper bag that peeked from the trash bin.

Gabriela tiptoed to the front door and turned the knob until the peg silently unclasped. She tiptoed down the front concrete steps, then crouched in the quiet of the grass. She peered through the front bushes at the skyline. *The sun isn't up yet, but there is light coming from behind those smokestacks. I think that's where we live.*

She started walking. *That way.* She tripped over a jut in the sidewalk. Gabriela shivered.

A car was coming. She scrunched the brown paper bag into an inner pocket of her coat and scrambled into the shadows.

The lone taxi drove around the block. Twice. Then slowed.

Gabriela ducked and held her position in a shadow. She didn't move, didn't even cross herself.

"Oh, dear God," she whispered in her best church prayer, "don't let me get hurt."

The taxi stopped on her side of the street, opened the rear door, and motioned to her. The man was brown. He didn't speak English.

She heard stern warnings from Abuelita in her head.

But she got in.

The taxi headed toward the river, toward the sunrise. The driver eyed her in the rearview mirror.

After some fifteen minutes, Gabriela grinned. *Here is the corner market. This is where Abuelita gets groceries.*

She gestured to the driver. He stopped near the front door.

She dove into the market. He didn't come after her to get money. *Maybe he is tired.*

He drove away. *Maybe he is an angel sent by God.*

The market was warm. Her breaths slowed.

A different woman than usual was behind the counter. *Maybe Abuelita is praying for me at the big hospital.*

* * *

Maia opened the apartment door quietly, hoping to restock the fridge before the little girl and Tanya heard her. She tiptoed into the kitchen. It was already 9:05 a.m. on Tuesday morning.

Later than I wanted. But hopefully, they slept in today.

She peeked at the couch where the little girl slept.

The couch was empty.

Maia listened.

No snoring from the bedroom.

Chloe tongued her fur and lay pristinely on top of the heaped-up blanket.

No little girl.

29

The aroma of the morning's fresh bread permeated the shop. Gabriela looked in her pockets. No money. Only the wrinkled brown bag with the hasty sandwich from this morning and the sticky orange from the club. And Abuelita's key.

Her stomach made a loud noise.

The clerk hazily glimpsed her way and headed to the coffee machine on the back counter.

Gabriela found some chips on the bottom shelf of the first aisle. *To go with the sandwich.*

And a candy bar. *For dessert.*

Gabriela carried her treasures to the milk case. She reached inside to touch a carton. She withdrew her empty hand and banged the glass door.

Quick. She slipped the candy bar into her pocket and scrunched the bag of chips into the elastic belt of her skirt.

She banged the glass door a second time.

Then Gabriela jaunted to the bathroom and turned on the faucet, left the water running, left the door open.

She snuck to the middle of the center aisle.

The clerk went to rescue the faucet.

Gabriela ran out of the door, leaving it banging behind her, jingles rattling.

She walked quickly, hiding in the shadows when she could. The apartments loomed many blocks down the street.

Gabriela came to the warehouses, with doorways where the drunks greet the morning. She crossed the street.

Finally, she reached the front door of the apartment building. Warm air hit her face. She scrunched to be smaller. *I still don't have a mask.*

A big person came out the door from the stairwell. *Stairs are better, anyhow.*

She darted through the door.

She climbed to the third-floor landing. The metal door on the third floor screeched open. A young Asian man scampered down the stairs, air whipping behind him.

He sighted Gabriela and grunted. The sound of his rubber soles echoed down the metal of the stairs and hit the gravel.

Gabriela looked up the stairs, litter hiding in the corners, cockroaches darting across the concrete. *Maybe the garbage man is sick too.*

Another flight. *I'm almost home.*

The apartment was locked. She found the key in her pocket and opened the door. A blast of stagnant air greeted her.

She locked the door, her shoes making tracks in a new layer of dust. She tucked the brown bag next to the coffee pot on the counter and hung her coat beneath her school bag.

I need to clean this place for Abuelita when she comes home. Is this the cupboard where she keeps the rags?

30

Dr. Ben needed a break by 10 a.m. He added three teaspoons of sugar with creamer to his coffee. *Tuesday, March 17th already.*

His phone pinged. The social worker, returning his call from yesterday.

Isabella's granddaughter is missing again. A bartender from a club found her Saturday evening, kept her over the weekend, and called Social Services yesterday morning. By yesterday afternoon, Social Services informed this person foster care had been located for the child.

But the child likely ran away, possibly earlier this morning. The social worker tried calling the child's school. But it is on lockdown and no one in the office can help. Yes, the social services department has notified the police of the missing child.

The social worker said the file on this child contained paperwork from a visit to the apartment yesterday, Monday afternoon. Neighbors claim no one has picked up the mail in almost two weeks. The landlord said the rent is paid until the end of March.

Frankly, the social worker confided, the neighbors were afraid of the virus. Since the grandmother had died of the virus, and the child had been with the grandmother, they were not willing, or able, to be of help. Plus, they spoke limited English. They came from countries where they couldn't trust their neighbors and they remembered the government as their enemy. They told social services they didn't know anything. Their eyes said they were hiding secrets.

Social Services hoped the child would reappear.

Yes, they were planning to visit the apartment again today.

Dr. Ben finished the call, interrupted his coffee, and headed for a solitary stairwell.

The door clicked behind him. He listened for noise above and steps below, then he crossed himself and prayed silently. For mercy for the child.

And mercy for himself—that Laura couldn't reach the attorney before he completed this rotation, before this epidemic, now pandemic, subsided. Attorneys were reportedly booked months in advance to take care of divorces.

Maybe the claimed uptick in divorces would end with the pandemic, when spouses were no longer isolated together. *Maybe delay could be an advantage.*

Dr. Ben rubbed his thumb on the handrail of the stairwell. *If I could just talk to Laura without her getting so angry she can't hear me. If only I had the energy to think of workable solutions.*

Laura and Ben had hoped this fifteen years of physician training would pass quickly. Then he would find a practice in a small town, where he would sit on the hospital board, attend school meetings, and coach soccer. Where there were four seasons, where he could sled down the hills with his kids in winter and water ski with his kids in summer. Where his patients would know him, he would know them, and he could walk with them through life—birth to death and all the in-between. The dashes on their tombstones, so to speak.

Now I'm stranded with at least one more year to go, during this horrible plague, unable to keep my marriage and family together. Is this worth it?

Everything he'd spent hours memorizing, that he studied to learn in medicine, wasn't working anyhow. The hours were, of necessity, longer than the eighty hours per week they'd promised.

Yes, I'm now a hero, which makes patients' physical attacks on doctors and nurses less likely. But this is still a high-risk job. Two doctors have already died from this virus.

I wonder how firefighters and police cope, knowing every time they leave for work, they may never be home again? Can they even buy life insurance? Whom do they designate as guardians for their children if they don't make it back from the next shift? Is every goodbye the final one?

He thought about Clapham. *How desperate do you have to be to end it all?* Why didn't Clapham choose something other than a gun? Guns are "canceled" by the medical establishment. *Not that any doctor or professor lives where you might actually need a gun.* But still.

Brains on the wall. Holy s—t! Couldn't he at least spare his kid that mental imprint? A priest somewhere in his memory told him that such solutions were a "mortal sin."

But I am a man of science.

Dr. Ben Lawson left the stairwell, grabbed his stethoscope, and strode to the ICU. He opened the laptop chained to the counter.

* * *

Science suggests the brain waves get disorganized. The MRIs of patients contemplating suicide show less blood perfusion in the frontal lobe where executive function should live. Poor thinking and tunnel hopelessness make suicide seem the only option . . . maybe suicide is just a brainwave malfunction?

What about Clapham's wife and kids? Kids who would grow up learning their dad killed himself. Will that make them feel valued? Will they grow up hating medicine?

Would life be worse for his kids if Laura really went through with the divorce?

Well, at least he could see his kids at their graduations and weddings. He presumed he would be invited.

Although—after that photograph from the side door of the club?

The screen turned blue.

I need to finish this note before the electronic health record turns off.

He put his head on the counter, arms folded.

I shouldn't be thinking such things. If I can just keep moving, working. Numb out all this craziness.

He looked up and hit the spacebar. The screen blinked to his last patient note.

I need to forget about Clapham. Will people think I'm weak if I get so desperate that I follow him?

31

A sudden rap on the door of the apartment. Gabriela startled and wobbled on her chair. Her cleaning rag drifted to the floor.

A lady's voice. Speaking Spanglish to another person. Gabriela's eyes scanned the room to the rag beside the cupboard.

Two more loud raps. "Is anyone home?"

Gabriela slid from the chair and tiptoed to hide against the wall.

She must not have a key. Not yet, anyhow. They might come back if the apartment manager gives her a key.

Gabriela gingerly pushed the chair to its place at the table. She listened for footsteps. None. She rescued her cleaning rag from the floor near the counter.

The sunlight shone brighter through the window.

Loud footsteps outside the door. A key was turning in the knob. Two turns, then a click.

Gabriela ran, cleaning rag in hand, to the empty trunk behind the bed in the bedroom. She positioned a blanket on top of the lid. She hopped in, then braced the lid with her hand.

Slowly. Slowly.

Softly.

Quiet.

She jiggled inside the trunk; she felt it snug against the bed. The soft folds of the blanket over the lid muted the unfamiliar voices in the kitchen. She put her hand over her mouth and nose. *Quiet.*

Gabriela could hear at least two people shuffling through the apartment. They were speaking English.

"Yeah, the lady who rented this apartment died over the weekend. That new virus is killing everybody."

"I thought there was a granddaughter who lived with her."

"Well, she's not here. She's only about five or six years old. Maybe she's with the neighbors."

Gabriela heard drawers slamming.

"Where did this lady keep her papers?"

Shoes echoed across the hardwood floors.

"Ah, here are some immigration documents and a green card for someone named *Isabella Zapota.*"

Rustling of papers.

"The apartment manager said the rent has been paid to the end of the month. Maybe the granddaughter will come back here for her things."

"Well, she's only about five or six years old. I doubt she'll understand."

Gabriela heard a gnawing from the corner.

Which corner?

The gnawing was getting louder, now echoing.

Sudden silence.

The people going through our apartment must have heard the rat.

Now whispers.

Maybe they don't know how to scare off rats?

Gabriela could hear them flurry near the door. "Nothing here."

"Rent is hard to come by these days," the younger voice commented. "Do you think we should let the manager know so they can rent this apartment out before the end of the month?"

"Let's wait and see if the granddaughter comes back. Let's give it a few more days."

The front door of the apartment slammed. The metal key turned twice and clicked.

Gabriela eased the lid of the trunk—just a slit. *Fresh air.*

She waited.

The hands of the clock are ticking in the kitchen.

No more voices.

She lifted the lid of the trunk and adjusted her eyes to the coming darkness. *They might come back if I turn on the lights.*

She tiptoed to the round circle on the wall. She turned it to the right. *This will make it warmer. But Abuelita says it will cost more money.*

She tiptoed to the counter. The crumpled brown paper bag was still there. Crumbs littered the counter. She looked inside. The sandwich was missing.

She felt her middle. The bag of chips was a lot smaller. *Little pieces.* The candy bar was still in her pocket. *Squishy.*

She found the orange, bruised and leaking, still in the pocket of her coat.

Gabriela dumped the bag of chips in the center of one of Abuelita's plates. She laid the candy bar on the edge. *Abuelita will be pleased.*

Gabriela put the orange at the center of the table. "Half of eating food is how it is presented." *That's what Abuelita says.*

Suddenly, she dropped her head to the table. *If only Abuelita hadn't left. If only she hadn't gotten sick and those men hadn't taken her away.*

Is Abuelita talking to God in Heaven to send me some money? I can't clean enough, even if I can get a job, to pay the rent. She had seen people sleeping under the bridge near the market. *Are they nice people? Is that an okay place? Will they let me stay with them?*

The wooden table vibrated. *Somebody is crying.*

Gabriela wiped the wet spots on the table with the sleeve of her yellow blouse.

She looked around the apartment, early afternoon shadows making scary monsters. *As long as that door holds and nobody else gets a key, I can stay here.*

Gabriela grabbed a blanket and headed for the trunk. *Away from the rat. And away from the people who want to rent this apartment to somebody else.*

* * *

An official invitation arrived via email from Health Sciences Administration at 2:10 p.m.

"Dr. Clapham passed away over the weekend and will not be returning to the team. Our condolences to his family. A memorial event is scheduled online for Thursday at 1:00 p.m.

"Mental health providers, social workers, and chaplains will be available online." Please click on the email link if you wish to attend.

32

I am sinister, a pretender. Devious, even demonic.

I am the spiny creature in the closet lurking to find you when you least suspect me.

Hiding, I disrupt systems, spew cytokines, and make clots where none should be. I kill doctors, patients, and dreams.

I am rearranging the futures of all creatures, not just those I infect.

I am unpredictable. They easily manipulated my image for political and career gains. I preclude the laws of nature and of medicine.

Just look at what I have accomplished in such a short time.

College campuses are empty, except for lurking killers and muggers, while students struggle to see beyond the blue lights in their bedrooms. Doctors struggle with inadequate supplies, logistical jams, and never-dreamed-of plans. Even when they have supplies, I defy the laws of predictability and baffle science.

Science is too slow to study me, and statistics are too obtuse to tell people what they really want to know. I will mutate and transform my image before they can capture me. I am the ultimate sleuth.

My greatest weapon is fear of me. Just think—cancel culture infects the entire world, including the world of medical thinkers, humans who are so self-assured they limit options, study obtuse ideas, and miss my weapons.

Well, they don't really limit my options. I will prove them fools, with weapons they can't see because they close their minds. Thinking themselves wise, they prove to be fools. They think their brains, awash in chemicals which they minimally construe with their diets, beverages, sex, and sleep—they think their brains will figure me out. But they are created creatures, just as I am a created creature. But my base has been here longer than they, and they are naïve.

I am the mongoose who has outwitted the cobra.

33

Repeated soft thuds hit the apartment door. Loud sounds—like squishy boots strutting back and forth in the hall, tossing packages against the wall. Voices enjoying a language Gabriela couldn't understand.

She heard metal, like a key, going round and round in the front door lock.

No click.

The sound of the boots faded away.

What if they come back with a key that works?

Gabriela jumped out of the chest and ran to Abuelita's dresser. She scooped up all the coins and the few papers of Abuelita's that those ladies missed. Then she grabbed a few of her clothes and her school backpack from its hook. She stuffed them in.

Then to the refrigerator—where Abuelita kept Pop-Tarts safe from the rat. Only one remained. Gabriela threw it on top.

She opened the door to the stairwell and squeezed through. *Can't pretend I'm a rabbit today.* She paused, silent, on the first step.

Two voices argued in Spanish several landings down. *They are heading down.* Their echo faded. *To the sidewalk.*

Her tiny frame hunched, shrugging the backpack over her shoulders.

She looked both ways, crossed the street, and headed toward the market. *I hope there is a different lady than yesterday.*

Her backpack slipped. Again.

She shrugged to get it over her shoulders.

There is a bridge here somewhere. A lot of kids hang out there, but I don't know if they like new kids.

She was suddenly surrounded by strangers, mostly kids. Some big, some little. Only one girl. They seemed to pass something among themselves.

One boy, taller than the rest, unzipped Gabriela's backpack. "Hey, turkey, you got any pellets for some Vanilla Sky?"

He grabbed the backpack and threw it to the ground. His face challenged. "Or are you into beans?"

Gabriela stood wide-eyed.

"Hey, little girl, you gonna join us?" The one girl finally spoke.

"Well, you little whore, you can spend the night if you smoke with us. And seal the deal." The group smirked.

"I have plenty of pellets." She turned to face them. "Not here, though." She tossed her hair.

"So where are they, little princess?" The group circled closer.

"Back at my place," she lied.

"Don't you go rat us out, you little whore. There's a police station three blocks from here," a second boy threatened.

"Well, we have a place too. We're moles, you know." The taunting boy pointed to hidden steps, heading down. "We live down there. We hide beneath the streets."

A man wearing a dark trench coat and a gangster-style hat appeared in the center of the underpass. *He is so big he fills the whole thing.*

The man looked her way.

A bus lumbered by, hissing loudly. It stopped for the red light at the next corner.

Gabriela grabbed the backpack from the center of the circle and dodged through the group. She ran a crooked line to catch the bus—frantic, her feet wobbling in her oversized shoes and her backpack bouncing side to side. But the traffic light stayed red for a long time.

She pounded at the rear door. The bus hissed; the door opened. She jumped the step to make it inside. The backpack landed midline along her spine; her toes pitched forward to make the shoes hug her feet.

Gabriela slowed to walk calmly, crossing the aisle and sitting behind the driver. *Away from his mirror.*

Her shaking fingers opened the backpack. The Pop-Tart was still there. Her clothes were still there. Abuelita's papers hadn't blown away. The coins still hid beneath them. She felt a mask near the bottom—from school. She put it on and kept looking at the door. *As if I'm waiting for someone.*

The bus tilted back and forth. Gabriela's head bobbed. She held onto the rail. *To keep my balance. Just like Abuelita did.*

Gabriela startled awake, then saw the sun dimming behind buildings outside the window. *The same buildings as before.*

The driver craned his neck to watch her in his rear-view mirror. He announced the next stop.

She zipped up her backpack, sat up straight, and waited for the next stop. *The back door will open with the front.* She skipped out the back, pretending happiness and a destination. The bus chugged to the next block.

* * *

She stalled on the sidewalk. No usual apartments. No corner store.

I must be lost.

But I need to pretend.

Gabriela spotted a shop with a neon OPEN sign. She skipped down the sidewalk to the front door, then waited for a big person to heave open the door. She slipped in the shadow of its closing.

There is an R on a sign near the back. She walked determinedly, opened the door, and went into an empty stall. Warm air blew from a vent near the ceiling. Gabriela hung her backpack on the hook behind the door.

Footsteps. Coming this way.

She jumped onto the toilet rim to hide her feet.

The door creaked open. Gabriela held her breath, her eyes glued to the mirror above the sink, the slit in the door held steady by the lock. A large woman tore a paper towel, wiped down the sinks, and turned the water knobs.

"Anybody here?" The woman's heavy breathing. "Last call for the night." The wad of paper towel hit the trash.

Gabriela held her breath and balanced.

The lady bumped the trash can.

The rumble quieted.

The door slammed, then a click. *Locked inside?*

Gabriela stretched inside the stall. The vent above her blew another blast of warm air. She put her coat on the floor. Then she laid down and listened.

No one seems to know I'm here.

She unzipped the backpack on its hook and cautiously opened the last half of the Pop-Tart. She let it dissolve on her tongue. A long time between each bite.

***

Dr. Ben headed to his home again. *It's Tuesday night. No need to bother with food, though. Laura and the kids is still in Florida with her parents.*

I need to find the key to the safe. Are there any bullets with the gun?

Maybe Laura stored them in a separate place. *I've never asked where she keeps such things.*

He shuddered. *Hopefully, away from the kids.*

The garage door closed behind him. *Should I just let the car keep running?* His legs relaxed to sit behind the brake and the accelerator. *Numb from standing on concrete floors all day at the hospital.*

Do I have enough energy to turn the key? Maybe I can just sleep in the car? Keep the motor running for just a few minutes. To keep warm? Maybe more?

Does it even matter?

In the smog of fatigue and carbon monoxide, Dr. Ben's brain drifted, then focused on eyes between the curtains to the left of the stage. *The club. Whatever happened to that kid?*

I need to stay alive to at least talk to the social worker one more time.

That is the one decent thing I can still do.

34

Footsteps outside the door. Boxes scuffing in a back hallway. At least two voices, muffled.

Gabriela felt the sides of the toilet, jumped to hang her coat beneath the backpack, then perched on the rim. Morning light shone through the row of clear cinder blocks that topped the side wall.

A key turned in the bathroom lock. The door groaned before a blast of air. Gabriela clung to the sides of the toilet and closed her eyes. *Lights on.*

A person whistled toward the mirror, tore paper from the dispenser. Gabriela could hear a wad hit the trash bin. The door closed and the sound of the footsteps went away.

Gabriela gingerly let herself down, lifted her backpack, and rearranged the items. She slipped on her coat, unbolted her cubicle, caught drips of water from the sink, and dripped her hands dry. She eased open the *R* door.

She headed into a shadow in the middle aisle. The fluorescent bulb above her buzzed, then flickered. Then went out.

She squinted to see in the new darkness.

In the gray, a large figure obstructed the aisle.

"Hola, bonita señorita," a male voice challenged. "Are you afraid?"

Gabriela gasped. *A man in the shadows.*

Pause.

She dropped her backpack and straight-lined toward the door.

The end of the aisle was filled by an enormous woman with curly hair. Gabriela could see only huge thighs and swaying breasts as the woman lunged to block the passage.

"She's afraid," the lady said in English. "I'll bet she's hungry."

"Well, our church has breakfast this morning," the big man said.

"Even with the virus?" questioned the big lady.

"Especially with the virus," answered the big man. "You don't think the virus took away the appetite, do you? Folks gots to eat, and with no monies comin' in, they be hungry."

In a blur, Gabriela walked down the sidewalk beside the gigantic man. She had never seen a man so big. She had never seen an angel, either. He had her backpack in one hand and her hand in the other. They walked toward a cinderblock building that smelled like fried bacon and pancakes.

* * *

So much food! It smells so good! I wonder if Abuelita in Heaven has this much food?

Gabriela stood in the short line, her eyes wide, a new mask hiding her smile. That big man heaped eggs and hash browns and a pancake onto her plate. He added a strip of bacon to the top.

She followed him to a table. She heard lots of Spanish. Not her Spanish, but she could understand what they were saying. Words like Columbia, Venezuela, Cuba, and Mexico. *Everybody seems to be from somewhere else.*

One or two of the women, likely mothers, looked at her with sad eyes. *They seem friendly.* Their kids finished eating, ran around, chattering in Spanish with bursts of English.

The next table had some people *with really black skin*; they spoke languages Gabriela couldn't understand. *They seem sad. But smart, like they have been on their own for a long time.* She watched them.

Near the end of the meal, the big man walked to her table and sat across from her.

"Little girl," he started, "what is your name?"

"Gabriela," she stammered. *I'm not sure I should tell my name.*

"Do you have a last name?" he asked.

"Zapota, I think." She twisted her mouth. "My grandma was named Zapota." *This man may be bad.*

"And where is your grandma?" he asked, his eyes kind.

"She went to Heaven. She got the virus and she went to Heaven." Gabriela looked down.

"And how long ago did she go to Heaven?" he asked.

"I don't know. I think it was about five days ago. I heard ladies talking about it."

"What ladies were talking about it?" He raised an eyebrow, and a lady across the table perked up.

"I don't know. Some ladies came to the apartment and they said that the lady who rented this apartment died."

"And where were you while these ladies talked?" he asked.

"In the trunk where they couldn't see me. A rat scared them off." Gabriela let out a breezy breath and raised her shoulders.

"So when did you last stay in the apartment?"

"I don't know. I think it was two days ago. It's hard to stay out of the way when you can't go to the apartment."

"What happened to your mommy and daddy?"

"I don't know."

"Do you have any brothers or sisters?"

"I think so, but I don't know where they live or how big they are." She looked worried, glancing around the room.

"Do you have a place to stay tonight?" The man looked at the woman.

"Oh, yes." Gabriela stood up, standing as tall as possible.

"Well, I think you'd better stay on my couch where it's warm until we find another apartment for you." The lady had a warm, kind voice. *Almost like Abuelita. Maybe she looks a little like Abuelita. Except, she isn't brown.*

"Where do you go to school?" the lady asked.

"I don't know the name of my school. It is closed now." Gabriela took a deep breath to make her chest big. "But I can show you it when I see it." *What if I can't remember what the school looks like*?

The lady walked over to the trash can. She punched the screen on her cell phone. When she returned to the table, she told the man that the Social Services Department was taking only phone messages. She said she had left a message to please return the call as soon as possible.

Gabriela left with the lady. They walked a long way, the lady holding her hand. Then they took the bus.

The lady had a couch. Just like she said. And—

"A puppy?" Gabriela dropped her backpack.

The dog wagged a bushy tail and leaned into her hand. "He sure has nice brown fur."

Gabriela pulled back to look at the dog's face. "And he has brown eyes. Just like me."

She looked at the lady. "Can he sleep with me?"

The lady nodded.

Gabriela squealed in delight, a sound that started in her toes and vibrated through her belly to her throat.

* * *

Thursday, March 19, 2020. Skipped lunch for this 1 p.m. meeting. Dr. Ben Lawson stood in his full protective gear outside the ICU and studied his phone as if it would ping for another call, hiding his reticence that an online memorial event for Dr. Clapham would sort his confused thoughts. His phone showed the tearful family, children masked and struggling to stay seated. Kind words exited the microphone, sniffles hidden behind the mandated masks. A few colleagues came onto the gallery view, numb to grief, taking a break from seeing patients.

A facilitator walked to a podium, mask on face. *He isn't involved in direct patient care. How could he know?*

Dr. Ben studied the gallery view, the faces of family members partially hidden by masks, some with face shields. *It's unclear who this is helping.*

He adjusted his PPE to enter the ICU. His phone finally pinged. The social worker said Isabella's granddaughter was still missing. However, a lady from a church feeding program had left a message regarding an unaccompanied child that fit her description.

35

Maia swerved the driveway to Shelby's house. Another holiday at this place.

This one while sneaking from government lockdowns, fearful of catching the dreaded virus, fearful of becoming a leper in the ever-changing government recommendations.

Maia cut the motor, frowned at her backpack thrown to the passenger's seat, and put on her mask.

"Well, social distancing hasn't canceled Easter lunch at Shelby's. Earlier this year—April 12, in fact."

She opened and slammed the trunk, carting her contributions to the meal. Sweet potatoes with walnuts and cherry pie from the bakery.

A masked Shelby answered the door. "Need to remind us to wash our hands. Government instructions, you know." Shelby headed for the kitchen, laden with Maia's cherry pie and sweet potatoes.

"Government instructions were to isolate at home," Maia mentioned into her mask.

She hung up her coat, adjusted her black turtleneck, and pulled her high boots over the cuffs of black leggings.

Shelby glanced from the kitchen. "You wore black? For Easter?"

Maia ignored her.

"Where's Dana?"

"In the basement." Shelby cast a look of caution. "Jeremy is here."

Shelby furrowed her brow toward Maia. "How are you?"

Silence.

Shelby flicked on the oven light. "I mean, honestly, how are you?"

"Fine," Maia lied. "Still making the rent. Haven't had to crash at Mom and Rasheed's place yet."

"Help me set the table." Shelby handed Maia napkins and silverware.

Maia started tucking napkins beneath the silverware.

"Nice day, isn't it?" Shelby kept moving.

Maia continued tucking napkins.

Shelby tried again. "Does anything you brought need to be refrigerated?"

"No," Maia retorted.

Shelby retreated to the kitchen and peered into the lighted oven. Her two kids argued loudly from the outgrown toy room.

Lisa and Rasheed sashayed through the front door, sporting matching masks.

Maia came around the partition. "Stylish masks, Mom. Might as well make fashion if we're not going to isolate at home."

"Sorry if we're late. We just finished online Easter services from the office at home." Lisa balanced on one foot, scalping off the other boot.

Rasheed arranged his shoes neatly beside the front door. "Didn't miss much," he mumbled beneath his mask.

"Busy trying to catch up at the apartment," Maia offered. "Having a cat means I have to keep the place vacuumed."

Rasheed lifted his mask and blew his nose.

"Fortunately, the cat isn't here," Maia smiled. "Your allergies are safe."

Shelby dried her hands on the towel rack. "Everybody, come wash your hands for dinner."

Maia winced. *Everybody follows Shelby's orders. Just like they always have.* She headed for the bathroom sink.

"Dinner's almost ready. I have tables and chairs set up in the garage," Shelby yelled from the kitchen. "The heater is on. It should warm up soon." She chauffeured the ham to the middle card table in the garage, already plastered with scalloped potatoes, beet salad, and fresh rolls. "Somebody call Dana."

Shelby's husband, Greg obliged her and yelled down the stairwell. A clock ticked above the sink. Twenty-five seconds.

Dana staggered up the stairs in his gym shorts and t-shirt, hair rebelling. "Jeremy's not coming."

"Does he think it's too soon to be meeting as a group? As a family?" Shelby frowned.

"No, he's not feeling well." Dana looked anxiously toward the garage. "Nothing like the virus—he's stretching his Suboxone until he can get an online prescriber."

Dana started walking toward the table in the garage. "Some dining room you have here," he teased.

The family assumed their usual seats, careful not to upend the makeshift tables laden with Easter traditions. Mom at the head of the table, Rasheed to her left, Maia to her right, and Dana next to Maia. Then Greg. And finally, Shelby at the end, facing Mom, her two kids flanking her side. Empty chair and place setting left for Jeremy.

Mom and Shelby managed a shaky duet of the perfunctory grace. Maia sat, head bowed, lips rigid.

Scientifically impossible! Someone being raised from the dead? Good luck with that one.

Shelby rearranged her napkin on her lap. "How about this weather? Warmest spring in about ten years."

"Well, it's not too warm here." Rasheed sniffed again.

"It'll do." Maia peeked at Shelby. "The heater is on."

Rasheed passed the scalloped potatoes to Maia. "How are classes going, now that the university is closed and all classes are online?"

"Well, we're less than six weeks into online classes. But it's the same old subjects." Maia nodded at the plate of ham heading her way. "Same old buzzard professors. In fact, I'm surprised they could adapt to teaching online."

Rasheed pocketed the beet salad in his cheek. "Teaching online takes a lot of planning and reorganization. I've converted the guest room to an office at home. It looks nice. Lots of plants."

He studied Maia. "Maybe you could find a job tutoring grade-schoolers, helping kids keep up while their parents work from home?" He rearranged his salad, a wry smile tagging his lips. "How good are you at activities to keep them occupied? I've heard online schooling leaves considerable free time."

Maia looked at Greg. "I see your neighbors have a new garage door."

"Yeah," Greg managed his mouthful of potatoes. "They got it done on a warmer day. Up and down temperatures since December." He swallowed. "Odd year."

"Odd virus," Maia added. "Seems to have the medical experts baffled, anyhow."

"Yeah, I wonder if it came from a bat or a pangolin? Or a lab?" Greg forked another scalloped potato. "Who knows?"

Maia laid her napkin in her lap. "The news said it came from a pangolin at a wet market, likely in Wuhan."

"Time will tell. Maybe it mutated from a bat." He grinned at Maia. "Maybe it's a bioterrorist agent from a lab?"

Maia nudged her water glass closer to her plate. "That's crazy! You're an engineer, after all. The news said it came from a wet market. You need to follow the science."

"Science is a tool. Only a tool. It'll take two years, minimum, to really understand this virus." Greg laid his fork, prongs down.

Maia stood. She marched down the hall toward the kitchen. She returned with small plates and the whole cherry pie.

"Anybody care for ice cream with their pie?" she asked airily.

Hands went up.

"I just made fresh coffee, if anybody wants some," Shelby offered.

Everyone's eyes followed Maia, returning this time with a gallon bucket of vanilla.

Maia slipped Lisa an Easter card. Lisa beamed.

Shelby fumbled a dented envelope from the pocket of her apron.

Dana poked his leftovers with his fork.

Pie and ice cream melted into mouths and paper plates. The big screen TV blared from the recreation room.

"No ball games today," Lisa chirped. "There were a lot of online Easter services this morning."

"Fortunately, they're over." Rasheed pushed back his chair. "No reruns needed, please."

"Time for some celluloids." Dana moved the leg of his chair. The concrete floor screeched. "At 2 p.m., we can see Judy and Fred dancing in 1948; then we can enjoy Ingrid and Humphrey trying to forget their tryst in Paris while they escape their wartime enemies."

Dana waved his hand, a twinkle in his eye, and took a bow. "If we hurry, we might see the end of the Easter Parade."

"I heard the Easter Parade in Manhattan is canceled due to the virus," Rasheed reminded.

"Don't remind us. We'll have fun, regardless." Lisa started for the recreation room.

The garage-turned-dining room emptied.

Shelby stashed a load of paper trash into the curve of her left arm. "Kids, can you carry something into the kitchen, please?"

The twosome tumbled over each other, clanging silverware into the sink. The television volume increased. Shelby picked the dishtowel off the rack and slung it over a sagging shoulder. She started rinsing pots and pans. Hot, steaming mist made streams run down her cheeks. She looked down the hallway. The ham, beet salad, and casserole of scooped out potatoes stared at her from the middle card table in the garage.

* * *

At the first commercial break, Maia stood. "I need to get home. Have to work tomorrow." She gave Dana and Mom the recommended elbow bumps and grabbed her jacket. "Leaving so early?" Shelby cast a tenuous glance from the kitchen.

"Yep." Maia was almost out the door.

"Call me if you need anything," Shelby yelled above the steam of scrubbing pots and pans.

"That'll be a cold day in hell," Maia scowled into her mask.

36

The "cold day in hell" happened at the end of the sidewalk. A remnant of old ice, hidden in spring dirt and melting in the early afternoon sun.

You have got to be kidding.

Flying. *Oh, no, you don't.*

Maia face-planted in the gravel. Her right knee twisted beneath her body, the torso heavy with Easter lunch.

Acid refluxed into the back of her throat.

"Oh, oh, oh—my knee," she moaned.

She gulped for air.

Maia brushed the gravel off her nose and chin. She lifted her head to scan the house for signs of help. Blank windows. *Not even somebody to poke fun at me!*

Tingling skin. A tear in the leggings. *Oh, no! My favorite black leggings.*

"Oh, my knee." *Definitely deeper than a scrape.*

She looked at her palm. *No bleeding from the hand, at least.*

Tried to move her flexed knee—*can't straighten it.* Tried to stand on one leg—braced her fall back to the ground. *I need at least one crutch.*

Maia looked back to the house. *Still nobody coming. Can this day get any worse?*

She snaked her body across the damp gravel, fumbled in her pocket to find the keys, and hoisted herself to the driver's side mirror. She grunted the jeep's door open and twisted her body into the driver's seat.

The right hand can shift from Park into Reverse. The left foot can dampen the brake backing out of the driveway. "Good thing this jeep has an automatic transmission." *Then to twist the bod so the left foot can manage the accelerator and brake if needed.*

Creeping home. *Fortunately, today is Sunday and a holiday. Not much traffic.* "One advantage to these lockdowns."

Maia managed the gravel driveway. Now to brake short of the garage door. *How am I going to get up the steps and into the apartment? Can my butt hold open the screen door while I get the key into the knob?*

She quit the motor and patted the backpack for her phone.

A text: "Tanya, can you come help me? I fell at Shelby's and can't walk."

Maia looked at the dashboard clock and hugged her jacket to her neck.

Six minutes. *Maybe I should call instead of text?*

Suddenly, Tanya appeared at the door, a new guy in tow. He bounded past Tanya, down the stairs. He soon had his nose pressed against Maia's driver's window.

She motioned. He backed away.

Maia pushed open the door. She took the guy's muscular neck.

"Glad I could help," he chirped.

Maia raised an eyebrow. *Maybe this one is useful, anyhow.*

Maia hugged his neck until she reached the couch. He headed to the kitchen, opened the deep freeze, and started rummaging.

"Tanya, where are the frozen peas?"

"Don't ask me. I don't buy the groceries." Tanya's slippers padded across the floor. "But you can use whatever you find."

The Guy brought the peas for icing the knee, found the TV remote hiding under the couch, and pumped a pillow behind Maia's head.

Maia kept her knee flexed. She flicked on the TV.

The parade is canceled. But the Ingrid and Humphrey rerun should still be playing. She adjusted the bag of peas on her jackknifed knee.

If I can ice this knee and get the swelling down, then maybe I can get it extended. Then maybe this Guy can get me a splint.

She texted Lisa. "Landed on my knee in Shelby's driveway. Hurts a lot. Can I borrow one of your pain pills?"

She eyed the clock above the TV. Twenty minutes before the text back.

"Yep. Can you come get them? I'll be waiting."

Usual Mom. Doesn't realize I can't even walk.

Maia called to the next room. "Tanya? How about you take my jeep and go to my mom's place? I need to borrow some of her pain pills." *Maybe not the best idea to send a roommate with an unknown boyfriend?*

No answer.

Her fingers punched the text. "Shelby, I hurt my knee leaving your house. Mom has prescription pain pills. She texted I could use some. They're at her house. I can't walk to go get them. Can you bring them?"

* * *

Forty-five minutes later, Shelby knocked softly, then nudged the door open. Her eyes focused in the shadows, then roamed the room.

"Wow, Sis, how are you gonna make it to work tomorrow?"

"I don't have work until Tuesday." Maia tossed a pillow to the base of Tanya's bedroom door. *Tanya and the new Guy need to stay in the bedroom until after Shelby leaves. No comments, no criticism. After all, I pay the rent.*

"This couch looks pretty uncomfortable. Do you need me to help you get to a bed?"

"No, I just need the pain pills. If I wanted your help, I would have asked for it!" Maia sassed, her cheeks red.

"Okay, then. I'll be off." Shelby set a glass of water on the lampstand. "Call if you need anything."

Shelby headed to the door. "Or if you want me to be the one to help you."

Maia mumbled half a thank you and drank the glass of water. She cradled the flexed knee into as comfortable a position as possible and hoped for restful sleep.

* * *

The room turned gray, cooler with the dusk. The knee was stiffer. *The pain pill must have worn off.*

Maia worked her body into a sitting position. Pain in the knee. Pain in her head. *I feel cold.*

Her hand grabbed her lower abdomen. *Only how to get there? A pair of crutches? Mom likely has Dana's old crutches from his junior high football injury.*

"Shelby," Maia texted again. "Could you go to Mom's, get Dana 's old crutches, and bring them here?"

Maia heard a door creak. Slippers padded in the dark. "Tanya, can you help me get to the bathroom?"

A bigger shadow appeared and carried Maia to the bathroom, positioning her so she could drop her leggings and toilet. Big Guy closed the door behind him.

"Don't go," she yelled after the shadow. "I need help to get back to the couch."

* * *

Fifty minutes later, the front door scraped open. Shelby stood, with the crutches in one hand.

Shelby started turning knobs, adjusting the crutches.

"I guess I needed you sooner than I thought," Maia offered.

Shelby just kept turning knobs. "Let's see if these are the correct length."

Maia hobbled to stand up, one knee in fixed flexion. She lost her balance and caught the couch.

"Are you certain you shouldn't go to Convenient Care and get this knee looked at? I don't think these crutches are going to solve the problem," Shelby intruded.

Big Guy rounded the corner, his voice deep. "Yeah, that thing's bad. You can't even straighten your knee. You need to get it checked." He nodded to Shelby. "The car must still be warm."

Her eyes wide, Shelby quickly recovered. "If you'll help me get her to the car, I'll take her to Convenient Care."

Maia looked confused, her eyes drugged and cloudy.

Big Guy didn't wait. He lifted Maia into his arms and carried her to the car. Shelby grabbed the crutches and the door.

Big Guy placed Maia gently on the seat, reached to fasten her seatbelt, and carefully adjusted her mask. Her eyes moistened, her cheeks burned. *Big Guy is like the father, the brother I've always wanted.* She stared through the windshield. *It might be time to learn his real name.*

She was suddenly twelve years old again.

With Shelby, on the way to get medical help.

Just like the day I found out I had leukemia.

37

Amazing what the twelve-year-old brain remembers. *The arm looked too pale to give eight vials of blood.*

The doctor came in with the nurse. He sat on a stool across from Shelby. He said deadly words. "The blood smear shows a form of leukemia." Maia was only twelve years old, but she knew those words. One of her classmates had died two years earlier from what sounded like the same thing.

Maia didn't remember the rest of the visit. She remembered Shelby crying, then squaring her shoulders and acting adult. Shelby had just celebrated her eighteenth birthday.

Much was a blur. The medical record rarely included what the patient experienced. Only what the doctor or other medical personnel thought was important.

Maia remembered the pain of the bone marrow aspirations and biopsies, the lengthy, sometimes painful infusions. She remembered vomiting all night, her hair falling out in the shower. She remembered getting doctors' excuses for school, explaining to seventh-grade classmates why she sat on the sidelines in every sport, why she couldn't exercise in physical education classes.

Why she wore a wig or an old-lady-style scarf. Why her hair grew in wavy and a different color.

She could still feel Shelby holding her close; she could still feel warm tears soaking her scalp. Their mother visited twice—once during the first chemotherapy, once about six weeks after the transplant. Mom had given Shelby medical power of attorney to sign for the evaluations and treatments. When they came home, Shelby assumed care of the household, as well.

Maia still hated cold steel—*it reminded her of the steel of the vault, the radiation. More bone marrows, more infusions, the central line. Finally, a port. Fewer needle sticks.*

Maia's face contorted. *The pain of this knee is bad, but nothing compared with the pain of chemo mouth.*

Maia smiled. *Shelby had snuck Maia's favorite puddings beyond the nurses.*

This afternoon, Shelby drove in silence, the crutches balanced against the dash. Maia glimpsed Shelby's silhouette in the dimming light. *I wonder if she still does her devotions every morning. If she still prays for us even though we don't want her to? If Shelby still hopes that we will return to her God and become all she claims He created us to be?*

The sign for the Convenient Care lit up in the early dusk. Shelby slowed to make the turn.

I hate her religion, but I truly love Shelby.

* * *

Maia hobbled through the front door, signed the papers, and tested negative for the virus. She readjusted her mask.

The nurse practitioner ordered an x-ray. No fracture. *Internal knee derangement. Who knows? Ice, physical therapy. Time. Maybe further imaging later?*

The NP cleansed the locked knee with antiseptic, injected lidocaine, and waited. Then she maneuvered the knee, reducing it. She applied a knee immobilizer, scheduled an orthopedic appointment, and prescribed pain medication. Maia asked for three work excuses. She couldn't remember the names of her employers. But she needed three. The NP scribbled her signature after a brief message on three script pages.

Shelby pulled the car to the entrance. Maia hobbled in and threw the three work excuses on the dash. Shelby watched in silence, eyebrows alert above her mask.

Shelby stashed the crutches and slammed the passenger door.

The drive-through pharmacist passed a clipboard for the signature needed for the narcotic prescription.

Maia slept. Shelby drove in silence.

Big Guy was still at the apartment and helped Maia to the couch. Shelby placed water next to the pain pills on the stand, next to the TV remote. Then she left.

The knee immobilizer and the pain pills worked. Maia dozed until after dinner. Then she sat up, suddenly aware. *This thing is laughable. This will suck at the salon if it reopens. God knows how I'll manage six-inch heels with this contraption on! And there will be no dancing at the club. Do I even need a work release for that place?*

She contorted to reach the glass of water. *Tomorrow is Monday.* She could call that kid's social worker again. To see if they ever found her.

She grunted. *I certainly won't be working.*

38

Monday, 10:00 a.m. The cell phone dinged. Unfamiliar number, but the same prefix as the university.

What could they want? Hopefully, not more money.

"Hello, this is the comptroller's office."

The usual greetings. Maia adjusted her leg on the couch.

"Yes, we called. One of your professors referenced you as a potential employee for our fiscal planning team. It would involve considerable data entry. Would you consider applying for the position?"

The work could be from home with flexible hours, as long as the employee kept deadlines. The pay was less than her other jobs. Maia did mental math, calculating cost savings in gas, clothes, and meals. She could email the application today and start Friday.

Maia wanted to jump with joy. *Doesn't work well with crutches and a leg in a knee immobilizer.*

She texted Tanya in the bedroom to bring her printer to the main table. She needed a chair, a table, a laptop, and a printer. Maybe a pen. That's all.

She started a text to Shelby. *But Shelby will think this is a God thing.*

She paused. *I know better. After all, I have taken science and statistics classes. This is just a happenstance.*

She erased the text to Shelby.

I wonder who recommended me. Surely not the buzzard?

She texted Dana instead.

39

"Can I have the crutches back?" Lisa texted. "Rasheed thinks he's sprained his ankle."

Maia finished the orthopedic visit. *This knee is healing great.* Just a walking brace for another few weeks. *Amazing what minimal weight-bearing can accomplish.*

"Will bring them back this afternoon."

Lonely drive back home. Old haunts. Old high school. The mall shuttered, with its naked parking spaces.

Maia pulled into the driveway, azalea bushes sporting early May blossoms. The cracks in the sidewalk look deeper. *No recent rollerblading. No rollerblading with this knee, regardless.*

New finials about the roof. *Tokens to Rasheed's religious preference.*

Lisa answered the door, took the crutches, and ushered Maia into the foyer. Maia noted a new recession in the wall. Warm candles, recently dripped wax. A wafting fog of incense. Fresh flowers and slices of fruit prostrating before a solitary Buddha.

The image stared at her. *Doesn't see or hear or speak.*

"Rasheed just got some tea from his family in India. Want some?" Lisa lifted the teapot from the cupboard. "The best from Darjeeling, you know."

"Well, it shouldn't affect my urine drug screen, should it?"

"Wouldn't want to lose those jobs, now would we?" Lisa teased as the kettle steamed on the stove.

"Nope." Maia slung her jacket over a kitchen chair. "So, how is it, having more people at home?"

"Well, we don't see much of Dana. He eats and sleeps pretty much on his own schedule. Jeremy is here a lot."

"How's the online professorship going for Rasheed?"

"Oh, it's turned out great. Lots of work to set things up. But now, he has more time for meditation and self-reflection."

"And how has this been for you?"

"Well, I'm not going to the gym." Lisa lit her blunt. "It's closed, you know. And the delivery service keeps me indoors." She paused. "Don't even go grocery shopping anymore."

"Well, hopefully I can keep this computer job. I can work from home. The new term is *pajama job*—top up for the camera, boxers or less on the bottom."

Lisa smirked.

Maia continued, tentative. "The rest have to brave the virus and the weather. The rent is still due each month."

"There is talk about making landlords hold on the rent." Lisa rubbed the cherry from her blunt. "The marijuana dispensaries and the liquor stores are open. They're essential, you know."

"Strange pandemic. Wonder about all this. Wonder what the world will be like when we get through this."

"I'm not worried about it. We should be back to normal soon."

Maia sipped the tea. "Nice chai. I like the spices."

"Yes, Rasheed adds a little cardamon. That's his secret."

A clock ticked on the mantle. The room seemed smaller. Smoke from Lisa's blunt drifted across the canvas picture, a seascape, hanging above the kitchen sink.

Maia flashed to her childhood. *A cross hung above the sink. She often looked at that cross. Especially during heated conversations at meals. Usually late, after 9 p.m. When Dad got home from the hospital. Had any of this really mattered? To him? To anybody?*

Well, it mattered to me! To all of them. Dad leaving, Shelby getting married, Mom hooking up with Rasheed. Legally this time, of course. Better for the finances. Did Dana's transitioning have anything to do with this?

Maia stood up. "Sorry, I have to leave. I want to beat the rush-hour traffic."

I will decide. This will not matter.

"Beat the traffic?" Lisa raised her eyebrows.

"Old joke. No traffic now." Maia tugged on her jacket and headed for the door. "Thank Rasheed for sharing the tea."

She rapped three times on the basement door on her way to the jeep. *Poor Dana.*

And Dana's partner, Jeremy, has already missed prom because of the virus—can't take a gay date this year despite the changed rules. Looks like high school graduation may be online too.

40

Desai texted Maia. She was rescheduling her party. *But later than Jonathan said—this virus has interfered with everything!*

Yes, wear your mask, social distance until you get to the party. Then do whatever makes you feel comfortable.

Maia dressed for late spring. Glad to be out of the apartment. *Feels like 2019 again!*

A burned odor greeted her at the door. *Marijuana? Sage?* Cool spring air billowed the saffron sheers at the window, burgundy velvet panels huddling on the sides.

"About time you got here." Desai fluttered among her guests. "The others have been here a while—munching, toking, and testing the bartender's memory." She laughed.

The bartender winked at Maia. "We're having a Cat Scratch session at midnight, if you can stay that long."

"I'll start with a margarita tonight." Maia placed her ringless left hand on the counter. "I thought

Cat Scratch was a high school game. An entry-level game."

"Maybe catchup time?" He shifted her drink across the ledge.

Maia surveyed the room and headed for a circular couch nearly hidden in the shadows. And a muscular-looking guy.

Desai closed the window; the air thickened. The muscular guy headed toward a blonde across the room. The seat next to Maia was empty. A pudgy guy soon filled it. He claimed he had seen Maia at college. Maia couldn't recall him.

Midnight came quickly. Desai lit more candles about the darkened room.

The muscular guy stood at the head of the room. He introduced himself as Jackson. The others crowded around the circle.

Desai lay on the carpet, her head in Jackson's lap.

"Tonight, we are going to learn how we are going to die," Jackson started.

A nervous banter went through the group. Two guests left and didn't return.

Maia sat transfixed. *Wanting to know. Not wanting to know.*

Jackson started to rub Desai's temple and began the monologue copied from the internet.

"There was an old woman who had a cat."

After some three minutes, Desai lifted her shirt. No cat marks, no red scratches.

Julia was next. Jackson started his story. It ended with a crash outside the window and the message that Julia would die in a ferry accident. She lifted her shirt: two scratch marks. She laughed nervously. "Well, at least I won't die from COVID."

Desai took Jackson's place. She motioned Maia to lie on the floor with her head in Desai's lap. The rubbing started in Maia's temples. Maia yawned. *This feels like the beginning of a facial massage.* The mantra continued, then finished. She sat up. No scratch marks.

Maia lay down again. The rubbing and the drone of a new story started. This time about a cat in an alley.

Cool air swept the room. Maia shivered. Desai intoned, "You will meet your sisters when you die of natural causes."

Maia sat bolt upright. *I have only one sister.* Desai lifted Maia's shirt. Three red marks streaked across her back. Desai giggled in success. Maia struggled to her feet and lunged toward the couch. *This beer is messing with my head. Too long since I've drank any alcohol.*

The rest of the party passed with unspectacular results. Desai's black cat wandered through the group. Jackson was to be shot. The message didn't specify if this was in combat or during a drug deal gone bad. Some unknown guy was predicted to be killed in a car crash. Someone else died in a stabbing in the subway. Desai would live to be an old lady.

Julia swore to avoid ferry rides forever.

Maia taxied home at 2:30 a.m. and succumbed to inebriated sleep, her head covered by heavy blankets.

Her bedroom door was locked.

41

"You know a Dr. Ed Clarke?" The ferryboat captain quizzed his passenger.

Maia winced at the name tag on her coat. She blushed beneath her mask and flipped it. *Why do I even need a nametag to tutor high schoolers trapped at home, doing class on their computers? Well, it's May. They're almost done. But, come fall, is a tutoring job even cost effective, given the ferry ride across the river?*

"Nice man. Good doctor." The ferryman pressed on. "Heard he's still working during COVID."

Maia looked away. *No eye contact, no comment.*

"Too bad what happened to his daughters."

"Which daughters?" Maia blurted.

Frigid waters crushed and groaned. The wind flipped Maia's scarf.

"The twins." The man nodded knowingly. "Don't know if he had any others."

The ferryman swung his rotund body into the chair that faced the window. "That's what they said was best to do. From what I heard, even his church friends thought the same thing." His muddied reflection glared back. He adjusted a few knobs.

Then he swung toward Maia again. He leaned forward. "That kind of thing is legal now, you know. You saw how they lit up the World Trade Tower in pink a year ago January."

Maia said nothing. She stared ahead, then put back her head and closed her eyes.

"I was a cleaning aide, then. Many years ago," he mused.

The ferryman returned to the controls, facing the window. "Hope this job lasts through this pandemic. I'm getting too old to change again now."

The motor started the welcome churn before the disembarkment. Maia surveyed the seats behind her. She was the only passenger.

Her head turned to the EXIT light. She adjusted her mask.

She headed for the stairs, grabbed the rail, and skirted to the main floor.

Maia hit the sidewalk, then the street, avoiding any puddles reflected by the streetlights. She ducked beneath the awnings to avoid the drizzle.

A cold thought whispered that she had more sisters than Shelby.

42

Anmar's family came to New York twenty months ago. Their infant would be raised in America. She would not remember Uzbekistan.

His wife and three of his daughters started a restaurant and English classes. Anmar found work at a meat packing plant, moving sides of beef in a refrigerated train car. Twelve-hour shifts were hard on a 42-year-old body used to the softer life of an economics professor. But the family pooled their earnings to pay the rent for the apartment.

They were making their dream a reality. New country, new language, new jobs.

They had each other.

And hope.

Tonight, Anmar smelled smoke as soon as his feet hit the sidewalk above the subway. His eyes raced to his street. He turned the corner to see flames lighting the night sky above their row of apartments. Anmar started running, closer and closer to the sight of flames jutting over the number of their apartment. Sirens started far in the distance.

It takes the wife only thirty minutes to finish the patyr for the restaurant.

The flames licked higher. Anmar ran across the yard, dropping his lunch bucket, kicking tricycles out of his path.

I am only ten minutes late! Our last is so little she should already be asleep.

"Tashte, Tashte!" He pounded his palm against his forehead, still screaming.

He burst through the door.

Suction slammed the door behind him.

Anmar gulped at the licks of flame that darted up the stairwell. Exhaustion escaped into terror. Power beyond himself raced through his body.

"Tashte! Tashte!" He raced up the stairs, ignoring the smoke and the searing pain of flames that snared his clothes and burned his skin. *How can a man love a little girl as much as an oldest son?*

An arc of the fire now swallowed the stairwell. Anmar pounded on the bedroom door. It didn't budge.

He rattled the door. The lock held. *The wife must have locked it after the littlest one fell asleep.*

He cursed in his heart language and started kicking the door, sweat dripping from his chin, the fire growing hotter.

Anmar kicked the door again, giving full weight to his steel-toed boot. A brief crack in the casing. No light escaped through the crack.

He turned to his right side and heaved into the door with the full brunt of his strength. The door budged—and then retracted.

Mock me! If you dare! His face reddened. He clenched his jaw.

The crackles of the fire grew louder. He heard someone screaming outside in the distance.

Tears raced down his face.

The fire now illuminated the doorpost. *If I can just break through this door.*

He heard a siren in the distance. *Can't tell if the sound is coming this way.*

It won't get here in time!

Anmar backed into the other bedroom and took a running leap into the door, his left shoulder screaming with the hit. He roared in pain.

The door blew out of its frame and banged on the floor. Anmar plummeted, his chest to the floor.

Anmar swallowed what spit remained in his throat, then writhed with its cut-glass trickle.

He felt for the tiny mattress in the corner. *Empty.*

He started along the hot floor, grunting for air, choking in spasms. *Can't get enough air to scream. Can't stop coughing.*

The fire and smoke are winning.

He stretched his left arm above his head and shook his head into his armpit. *This heat! Any way to get air.* His right hand fell across his name badge.

He could see the faint outline of a prayer rug still rolled in one corner. *The Holy Quran must still be in its place.*

He bent his right hand upward to gasp, "Have mercy! I cannot get it."

He panted and rested, trying to pool enough spit to lick his parched lips.

If I can dream I'm swimming in cool water.

Anmar rolled his body and turned his arms for a breaststroke. He grabbed at the floor. He grunted his chest to move forward on the hot floor to the sideboard in front of what had felt like a tiny mattress empty in the corner.

His eyes stung with grit and tears. Darkness. *Hides everything.*

Anmar felt a lumpy softness—warm, curled, soft bones—*must be her.* He rolled her over next to him on the floor.

He heard a soft gasp. He grabbed the warm poking mass, tossed it over his shoulder.

There are no windows in this room.

Anmar grunted to his feet. He stumbled over licks of fire outlining the fallen door.

He reached the stair casing, flames nipping the charred legs still left from his uniform. *Are there any stairs left?*

His feet had learned from his childhood how to herd goats on rocky ledges. He scampered down the flame-licked charcoal of the stairway—sliding, riding what the fire had left of the banister. The smoke was a thick curtain, unforgiving, unwilling to move—acrid burning of his face, sweat beading on his forehead.

His boots hit a firm footing. He lunged right—*he hoped—to the ground floor door of the apartment.*

The door burst open.

Air! Precious air! Precious, chilling rain!

His upper lip was a waterfall of sweat and soot, and his lower lip was huge. *Maybe it can catch a few drops.*

Anmar winced. *The taste of drying blood. From my lips?* He tried to open his teeth.

Cloudy flashes of red and blue lights. Blinding headlamps. The stomping of boots.

He held the heavy trophy of the warm mass toward the first big presence that paused. Through eye-slits, he saw a blur of tiny red roses on pink flannel peek from a charred blanket.

More huge dark shadows. Shouts in English he couldn't understand. Scrapings, grunts, and huge hoses moaning across the floor. Water thrashing.

There was a pause in the shouting of the bodies. He managed to stumble to the door. His arms and legs couldn't move any more.

His body crashed into the icy concrete that melted into his face and chest. *Maybe this is as close as I will get to Paradise.*

* * *

"Trauma code, room nine, in ER," the overhead squawked.

Dr. Ben Lawson ran to the stairwell. *At least this is a departure from the virus.* His arms grabbed the rail, swinging his body to save time.

"I really must get to the gym," he huffed. "Maybe the next day off."

But going down is definitely easier than going up.

Dr. Clarke was already in the ER, striding toward room nine.

Dr. Lawson followed Dr. Clarke, intentionally narrowing his eyes. He swallowed twice, the nauseating smell of smoke and burned human flesh permeating the room.

A nurse cut scorched clothes off limbs that dangled over the stretcher. Soot outlined its base. The victim was a middle-aged man of Central Asian appearance. He was unconscious. A paramedic was bagging him using a facemask.

The man's eyebrows were virtually gone. His lips were swollen with dried blood beneath the mask, his upper lip black with debris. His hands looked charred. The skin from his right side fell in strips as the clothes were cut away. There was no blood to follow, only dots of clotted capillaries on a white background.

Dr. Ben compressed his lips below his mask. *Third grade burns. Skin grafts. If this guy survives that long.*

The nurse continued cutting off the clothes. "Anesthesia has been called, but they are delayed in the OR."

"Shouldn't you intubate this guy before his airway swells shut?" huffed the paramedic, his arms sagging.

Dr. Clarke took the position at the head of the stretcher. He muttered into his mask, "This guy has had enough smoke inhalation to need an expert to intubate his airway."

A lab technician approached the door, her mask hiding her face. "The COVID test on this patient has returned positive."

The nurse warned, "Anesthesia and the intensivists say there are only two more ventilators in the hospital."

Dr. Clarke glared straight ahead. "Regardless of COVID, this guy gets intubated soon. And he gets a ventilator, if possible."

* * *

Technicians were starting IVs, the central line kit ordered from central supply. The Quentin catheter was on standby. Dr. Ben shifted his feet. *This patient is likely to need dialysis when his kidneys turn bad. He has at least sixty percent body surface area burns and severe smoke inhalation.*

The firefighter paramedics chatted outside the door. They seemed amazed the man had survived at all. He had handed them a toddler just before he collapsed—apparently his youngest daughter, found in an upstairs bedroom. The patient had saved her life.

The child was being taken by a different ambulance to the children's hospital across town. She was unresponsive, but she had no burns. They were screening her for carbon monoxide poisoning. It looked as if she would survive. The rest of the family were still at the restaurant, as they provided carryout until 11 p.m. They were unaware of the fire. Unless they could stay at the restaurant, social workers would need to find a place for them to spend the night.

"Ben," Dr. Clarke barked. "See if anybody upstairs has a ventilator they can free up."

Dr. Ben Lawson tapped his phone, asking for the head nurse.

The ER nurse continued snipping, the clothes falling beside the stretcher.

Dr. Clarke turned to view the shivering body. "That little girl may never understand how precious she is to that man. Love will probably pay the ultimate price."

Dr. Ben stared at Dr. Clarke, then whispered into his mask, "Good Friday already happened on April 10th of this year."

43

The head nurse returned Dr. Ben Lawson's call. An elderly lady, currently hospitalized on the fourth floor "doesn't want all this fuss and bother" and was rescinding the ventilator by her bed. She wanted, instead, to go to hospice care.

A qualified person needed to speak with her and write new orders. She had a living will, but it was vague. No, she hadn't discussed her decision with her daughters, two of whom were out of state. Her son was her medical power of attorney anyway. With COVID precautions, he was available only by phone.

No, she hadn't discussed this with the chaplain or the social worker. The medical ethics committee was meeting online only as needed.

She just decided tonight. Although she was only eighty-four years old, she had enjoyed life and was ready to take the next step, which, for her, involved hospice and end-of-life care. No ventilator.

Dr. Ben punched the elevator to the fourth floor to discuss this with the patient and get the ventilator back to the ER as quickly as professionally possible. *Dr. Clarke is waiting at the head of Anmar's bed.*

Dr. Steinham caught the elevator at the second floor, carryout food and a beverage in hand. "Just like I said. Experts from all over the world are here, snaking their line through the ICU every morning and every afternoon."

Dr. Ben nodded. "Well, they're not here now." *Even giving up takes energy.*

Dr. Johnson, an old family practice doctor, practically retired, got on the elevator at floor three.

"I thought you would have gone home by now," Dr. Steinham commented to the older man and moved to hide his carryout.

"I can't seem to leave. Haven't solved the puzzle yet." The elevator shook. The old doctor grabbed the handrail.

"Well, maybe it'll come to you. I see your colleagues standing around the ICU, hands in their pockets, unable to leave." Dr. Steinham moved his carryout behind the sleeve of his unattended arm.

"We've never had an illness before where so many of the patients died. We can't leave. Not yet, anyhow." Dr. Johnson struggled to push his spectacles above the mask hiding the bridge of his nose.

"Well, one of our colleagues has already left." The elevator jerked. Dr. Steinham balanced his carryout without a spill.

"A shame to lose that fine young man." The old physician shook his head. "Bad for him, worse for his kids. Bad for the morale of the team."

Dr. Johnson blocked the elevator door on the fourth floor with his hand. He turned to Dr. Ben. "Patient care comes first, you know."

Dr. Ben Lawson nodded his thanks and whisked down the hall to find the lady.

He sat directly across from her, tried to understand her life's path in the brief time allotted, and got the phone number of her son. He also texted the chaplain. *Just in case.*

Dr. Ben excused himself to make a phone call, easing the ventilator out the door and to the staff elevator. He shook his head.

Visions of Dr. Clarke, gloved hands folded, at the head of the bed.

Room 9 in the ER.

Waiting.

44

Dr. Ed Clarke looked at the tired reflection in the elevator glass. He still had his mask on.

A haggard lady pushed a baby carriage onto the elevator, items tossed in the bottom *where a baby should have been.* The odor of the street followed her.

Lisa was suddenly beside him in the glass. *How can she be here? Is there such a clinical entity as COVID-caregiver brain?*

Lisa was barely twenty-four, her hair blonder, her waist smaller. She still had generous boobs, bigger today as her milk was coming in. Her enormous belly was now softer, slightly concave.

They stood in shock. Like stoic pioneers in an old photo. The doctor had said the twins were both girls but conjoined at the head. There was a neurosurgeon, out of state, who might separate them without killing either of them. But such a surgery was out of their insurance plan. It would cost a bundle. A referral call required their joint permission.

A man with a mask under his nose but over his mouth darted into the elevator at the third floor. Ed motioned him to put the mask over his nose.

The elevator hit the ground floor. The man got out.

Ed pushed a button, oblivious to the floor elevating beneath him. A faint ding heralded the eighth floor. The door groaned open and closed. No human traffic.

Ed punched number sixteen.

How could God let this happen to them? What had they done wrong? Had Lisa taken anything more than a rare acetaminophen the whole pregnancy? She hadn't even had wine with a steak meal, once the home pregnancy test was positive. It was simply unfair. God made things good, successful, and beautiful. He punished those who disobeyed Him. What had they done wrong? What should they tell their church, their groups? What should they tell their parents?

Ed and Lisa were good people. They were doing all the right things. Ed was a physician on the rise. Lisa was the beautiful darling, the career woman, the homemaker, the dream of every man. Deformed twins could not be.

This would not be.

The elevator dinged at floor ten. The doors groaned open and closed again. No human traffic. Again.

At first, they visited the newborn nursery. They glanced at the perfectly formed babies belonging to someone else. They hid their tears. After all, they were good people. It was a sin to be jealous of others. It was a sin to be mad at God. They pretended to be happy. They cooed and ogled and smiled at the nurses. They cast furtive glances.

Ed and Lisa never discussed how God had disappointed them.

The girls had blonde curls, beautiful blue eyes, every part perfect—except they were joined. Joined at the head. Lisa visited and cried. She tried to breastfeed one of them at a time, a nurse holding the other.

Lisa stopped talking to Ed about God things. She chatted about the weather, the busy travels of the in-laws, and the next family meal.

The elevator opened and closed at floor twelve. Ed was the only one riding. Nobody came or went.

Ed remembered that he visited for three weeks. The doctors had many opinions. The surgery would not be the first of its type. But it might fail. Who knew if they would be like stroke victims, paralyzed on the contralateral side? The social worker noted the girls would have scarred heads. Ed got the message: They would always be less than perfect; they would always have to adjust their hair and try to explain their beginnings to people who wouldn't understand. They might be too handicapped to explain this well, to even be "normal." Dateless prom nights and endless spinsterhood shot daggers into his dreams of happiness for them, for proud moments as a parent of society's successful children.

Ed decided against the surgery. By week three, Ed stopped pretending. He stopped visiting.

The elevator stopped at floor sixteen and buzzed. It was at its highest floor. Ed shook his head.

Lisa had cried endlessly. When Ed wasn't with her, Lisa didn't go, either. She said it was too painful. The twins' crying made her milk let down and her boobs hurt.

The babies were kept in an inner sanctum at the hospital. Only the cleaning staff went in there.

The milk and water were withheld. The doctors assured them this was painless, that ketones were their own anesthetic.

It took eight days for the girls to die. They stopped crying, became listless. The nurse told Ed and Lisa that they died within minutes of each other. The cleaning man told her so.

Ed and Lisa told their parents, their church, and their groups—even Ed's doctor colleagues—that the babies died from complications of the birth. The groups nodded that such was common in twin births. After nearly three weeks in the hospital, such endings were to be expected.

The babies were buried out of state, without a service, at the far corner of Lisa's family plot. Neither Ed nor Lisa attended the burial or ever saw the grave. Lisa had a simple marker, "The Clarke twins, girls," ordered to mark the grave. She told Ed that she called to be certain the marker was placed.

Ed punched button fifteen. There was an old man with a graying beard in the glass's reflection.

Every time they pretended love and every time they had a baby, which happened three more times, they felt a loneliness deep inside that chewed away their oneness. And after each pretense of intimacy, and after the birth of each baby, Lisa turned her back to Ed. He thought he heard a sniffle. He hadn't checked to see what it was.

He was still in training. Another fellowship, another long day. The nights were numb, exhaustion the final anesthetic. Yahweh and the Jesus of that church had lost any place in this equation.

When Dana was seven, Lisa found her professor more comforting than her spouse. The divorce had happened long before.

The elevator hit floor twelve. A different old man got on, mask in place. Lisa was nowhere to be found. She must have gotten off on an upper floor.

After Lisa married her professor, Ed lived alone. But he had financially helped many friends. Maybe these good deeds would balance the other?

The elevator made quick time to the sixth floor. *Who knows who pushed that button?* Nobody got on. The old man with the mask kept looking at him askance in the glass.

The next year Maia got her leukemia. *Nice effort, God! Trying to punish me more than I punish myself. I'm not playing this head game anymore!*

Ed clamped his fist. Inside his coat cuff, of course.

The elevator hit the ground floor. The cables groaned again. Ed wobbled with the shimmy. He grabbed the cold metal of the rail.

Ed shook his head. *If only my head will clear, I can find my way home. This clutter.*

The sun outside the glass elevator made shadows of the trees. That old man followed him out of the elevator, making shadows that mimicked Ed on the sidewalk.

When will people learn not to stalk you? Especially during a pandemic!

***

Ed caught three subways, then walked several blocks, to make it home. He hardly remembered what home looked like. The world outside the hospital looked weird, as if aliens had invaded and everybody was hiding behind closed doors and drawn windows.

That old man, however, had been lost in the transit.

"Thankfully!" Ed sputtered to himself.

He was heading home. "A taxi would have been faster," he complained.

New weeds sprouted around the house. He slammed the door and kicked off his shoes. *No one is home, regardless.*

He headed for the liquor cabinet, shot glass in hand. *Time for some aged whiskey.*

The cabinet was empty, except for two bottles of cheap wine, a third full. He left the glass on the counter and headed for the shower. *Hot water—such a reprieve.*

He passed his unmade bed. He dropped there. *Just to rest for just thirty minutes.* Before dinner.

Dinner wasn't planned. *Who knows, maybe the refrigerator is as bare as the liquor cabinet?*

I will take care of it when it next matters.

He drifted.

A sweet blonde head bobbed across the pillows. "Daddy, Daddy," the little-girl voice delighted. He slept on. Suddenly, moist but tiny lips were on his forehead, his ears, and then his cheeks. Kisses directly over the eyelids. He put heavy muscular arms around her tiny torso and pulled her under the covers. Her tiny ribs giggled as she snuggled close. It was unclear if she was cold. Her feet certainly were! They got warmer, though, as the minutes passed. He breathed deeply, somewhere knowing that this moment wouldn't last forever.

The deep and peaceful sleep lasted until 1 a.m.

He was suddenly awake, stumbling to the night-light in the bathroom, trying to find the master switch. The glaring red clock announced the ungodly time. *It is only four hours until I need to get up again.*

He caught his stumble on the rug in front of the hot tub. *Any doctor concerned with falls would ban that thing!*

He eyed the counter from the mirror's reflection. It was barren. *When did Lisa get rid of all her makeup? Where are all the hairbrushes, sprays, and perfumes?*

He listened for giggles, for video games, and TV announcers.

Silence.

His bare feet shivered to the tiled kitchen floor. He found a cold cup of coffee on the table. He sat down.

Where is everybody? Have they gone on vacation without me?

The calendar on the wall said it was 2020. A newspaper, partly crumbled, said March 2020.

I must have COVID brain. But I don't have a fever. The last time I checked, anyhow.

He shook his head, ran his fingers through his balding scalp.

Self-awareness is not my forte. But a grown man, sobbing on a kitchen table at 1:15 in the morning? *This is justification for most physicians to call a shrink!*

* * *

Ed texted his favorite psychiatry consultant. "I think I need a head scan and some medication. I'm having crazy dreams. Maybe I've been in the hospital with COVID patients too long."

The clock said it was before 2 a.m. *My favorite consultant is not answering texts. Likely isn't even on call.*

Ed punched the on-call operator. *This is a private matter. I don't even know who is on call for psychiatry.*

He heard two rings, then punched out.

He sat in the cold for several minutes. *Maybe the cold will help any brain swelling I might have.*

A soft tap hit the window beside the table. He listened.

Silence.

Three soft taps.

He went to the door.

A disheveled man, hovering under his hood with no mask, stood in the dim light.

He spoke broken English. "Baby needs milk. Wife sick. Walked a long way."

It was cold outside. Ed let the man in.

It may have been a trance. Ed found his slippers, drove the man a long way to a corner market, gave him twenty dollars cash, waited in a warming car for him, and drove him to a tenement apartment in the inner city. He counted five twenties from his wallet and handed them to the stranger as the man grabbed the sack with the baby's milk and got out of the car. The man thanked him profusely and seemed sincere, despite horrid teeth and putrid breath.

Ed returned to the house at 5:30 a.m. and exchanged his slippers for work shoes. He changed his clothes and appeared, he hoped, unscathed for morning report. *I wonder how many dreams I had last night?*

But he was missing one hundred and twenty dollars from his wallet. And he was hungry. *I must have missed dinner last night.*

45

Dr. Ben Lawson scrolled his computer. Another death certificate in his queue. This one for Anmar. *I hadn't recognized his real name in Uzbek.*

He heard breathing over his shoulder.

Dr. Ben turned.

Dr. Ed Clarke gestured time out.

"You know that patient had a positive COVID test," Clarke reminded.

"Yeah, but he died of his burns. The COVID test is done on everybody who comes into the emergency room." Ben paused his typing.

"And mention that he was on a ventilator," Clarke directed.

"But he was on the ventilator for smoke inhalation, not COVID," Ben argued.

"We don't know that for certain. Yes, he had smoke inhalation. But maybe he was also getting pneumonia from the COVID."

Dr. Ben interrupted the death certificate. He scrolled through his inbox.

Silence.

"Just be certain you mention both—the COVID and the ventilator—in the cause of death. It may make a difference in reimbursement for the hospital."

Dr. Ed Clarke tore off the yellow paper gown and turned to leave. "How else can we take care of these indigent patients with no insurance? The hospital needs to make money somehow. The government subsidies don't cover our costs." Dr. Clarke adjusted his mask. "This isn't a free lunch, you know."

Dr. Ben flicked through the labs listed on the computer.

"You people need to take a course in economics. Learn how the system works."

Dr. Clarke marched out of the ICU.

46

"Oh, my aching head!" Shelby couldn't smell the chicken frying for lunch. She paused, salt shaker in hand. She couldn't taste it, either. *Was it already too salty already?*

While the chicken simmered, she would get the dishes out of the dishwasher. *Very short of breath.*

Shelby looked at her fingers. *Bluish purple.* She checked her toes. *Same color.*

She made it to the bathroom. The thermometer read 103.6.

She punched Greg's button on her phone.

He didn't answer. *Must have snuck to the grocery.*

Shelby turned off the stove and managed to get herself into the car, into the clinic, into the waiting room. She closed her eyes and waited for the rapid COVID test. *Positive.* The nurse reported her pulse oximetry as 83%.

She texted Greg. "Positive COVID test. Being sent by ambulance to the hospital."

* * *

The ambulance was frigid. Bumpy. Shelby's hips banged against the stretcher, her arms folded and strapped against her chest. Warmer air blew on the side from the overwhelmed heater, but cold air streamed under the back door. Some kind soul placed a warm blanket over the stretcher, the vehicle swirling in traffic, its tail gyrating.

The ambulance jerked to a stop, the paramedics jumping to their positions, the stretcher again strafed by the wind. Retching. Blanket to her mouth, curled like a fetus. Oxygen tubing torn away.

Yelling. Noise. Boots on metal. The nurse adjusting the mask across the bridge of Shelby's nose.

"A sister has been calling repeatedly. Trying to find this patient. Maybe a quick phone camera time will halt the calls." The nurse grabbed Shelby's phone and punched buttons.

Maia turned her phone sideways, increased the volume. The picture appeared. "Are you certain this is the correct patient? She looks really old. Not herself. I can't understand what she's trying to say."

Flashing red lights and buzzers interrupted the call. "This patient's pulse oximetry and blood pressure just plummeted," the nurse yelled as she hastily set the phone on the counter.

Another nurse ran into the room with a different mask, larger tubing.

Shelby punched the air and tore off the mask. "Give my sister the note in my purse. And my phone." The newer nurse panicked to replace the oxygen.

The camera continued to image.

Four space figures with masks, yellow gowns, shoe covers, and two pairs of overlapping gloves entered the room. They lifted Shelby onto a bed, strapped her in place, and hit a button. She proned like a pig on a spit. The four figures left.

Maia gasped into the phone.

Shelby is fat, out of shape, and has outdated beliefs, but they could at least give her the courtesy of treating her like a person.

She punched the number to the hospital front desk.

"My sister was just admitted to your hospital. Just before they rolled her, she told the nurse she wants me to have her purse and her phone."

The answering person stated he needed to check with Security.

47

Shelby sank into the soft warmth. Weightless. Airy, and floating to the ceiling. Her obese body lay below her--the sheets hurled back, the body naked. Shelby looked down from the light fixture at the nurses and doctors scurrying to intubate and chest compress her body.

They're not asking me anything. They act like they don't know I'm up here.

The surgical lamp below her didn't hurt her eyes. She looked up.

A familiar bearded face greeted her. His eyes twinkled. "Well done, Shelby," the bearded face smiled. "Do you want to come home now?"

"Yes, that would be wonderful," Shelby sighed. "In fact, a relief."

She felt whiskers on her cheek, her person restored by caressing warmth. Perfect seeing. Perfect hearing. Perfect understanding—life's craziness had no consequence. Gorgeous music. Flowers radiant in deep colors.

The complete area dazzled, like a dew-dropped earth glistening in light, breathing fresh ozone after a rain.

The gentle smile was hopeful. “You need to go back.”

Shelby protested. “It’s lovely here—truly beautiful. I want to stay.”

“Yes, I know.” The bearded man’s eyes were kind but firm. “But you have more to do. You need to go back.”

The body groaned with cold. The blinding surgical lamp made the head scream.

Skin pain. A tingling shot up her arm. Her entire being gyrated, feeling pinned to a carpet whirling in a tornado.

Her voice box screamed in pain, unable to speak, unable to protest.

The world continued its nauseated heaving. Cold sheets, a lumpy, deformed bed. Voices outside her head, calling for heavy sedation.

Another insect sting in her belly. Mumbled talking.

If only she could groan. *I must focus on something.* Voices calling for tape for her eyelids and straps for her hands.

I need to talk down my panic. Air hunger. *That tube isn’t giving me enough air.* She rallied her few remaining, the few brain cells that would still think. *I have to remain calm. But I am drowning. In deep water. I am trying. Flailing. Sinking. Going down. Down. Down. Darker.*

She tried to remember the bearded face. His presence was holding her hand. His hand was warm and firm. Steady.

She tried to grip it, to let Him know not to let go.

But her hand went limp. She couldn't hold on.

The warmth of the bearded man's hand closed around her wilted fist.

A bizarre hope: If this bearded man could hold on and just keep her hand warm, she might get through this alive.

Nothing.

48

"Shelby has been sick for three days and finally went to a clinic. She tried to call, then finally texted," Greg explained. "Her test for COVID is positive, and her oxygen is low. They're sending her via ambulance directly to the hospital."

Maia pressed for details.

Greg was his usual engineering self. Truncated. He would "know more later."

Maia paced. "I've already called them. They let me see her on the phone camera. The call was interrupted when her oxygen got lower. They're working on her now. I think I need to go there."

Greg spoke in a controlled voice. "The hospital receptionist told me not to come. I can't get in, anyhow. COVID precautions. I'm heading home. The kids will have a lot of questions."

Like I don't?

She heard his truck shifting gears.

"Can I do anything?" she pleaded.

"Well, you could pray. But I know you don't believe in that anymore." Greg's truck protested another shift in gears. "I suppose you could go to another party."

"Desai's party is only a party."

"Party or seance. It's your choice. If you consider the Dark Side a reliable source of information."

Maia heard Greg's tires hit gravel. *Likely his driveway.* He cleared his throat.

"But if you really want to help, you can go with me tomorrow to get Shelby's van out of the clinic parking lot."

Maia hopped in her jeep and started to the hospital. *I know I can't go in. I'm not even listed as the next-of-kin.*

"But I can be near," she announced to the windshield.

She pushed on the accelerator.

Maybe I can get her purse and the phone.

***

Maia waited in the jeep for over four hours. Her phone pinged. The receptionist claimed to have spoken with at least three other personnel. Maia could come to a side door to get the purse and the phone from Security.

Maia adjusted her mask. She ducked into her parka hood per the spitting snow and ventured through the jeep flaps to the front door of the hospital. The security man asked who Maia was, wanted

ID, then handed her a plastic bag, crammed with Shelby's belongings.

"Good God," Maia spat. "You'd think Shelby was a leper! Is she really spreading COVID like red pepper on a white napkin?"

Maia skidded on the layering snow to the jeep. *It's May 9—a little late for snow.* She hoisted herself into the driver's seat and reached for the knob controlling the windshield wipers. *But snow landing on the windshield?* Maia interrupted her reach and watched the snowflake onto the glass. *Privacy.*

She opened the purse. At the bottom was a tiny book, hiding a serrated notebook leaf, torn from a spiral. The edges were ragged, yellowed. The message looked old. It was dated 2011, when Maia was twelve years old. The original was nicely scripted in pencil.

"Dear Maia, I remember the first time I saw you. The doctor allowed me in the room for Mom's routine ultrasound. The technician put more gel on Mom's tummy, and I saw your tiny face on the screen. You had the most adorable nose, a beautiful profile. We could see your spine. Your tiny heart was fluttering. I fell in love with my younger sister that day. I never guessed that you would get leukemia and that I would be a close enough match to give you stem cells.

"Today, when you spend hours alone in that steel place, with radiation destroying part of you, you will not be alone.

"Remember, God has you carved in the palms of His hands. He made you; He has a purpose. No matter how disappointed we may be, He is carrying us. Since He is the one doing the carrying, He determines the path.

"I'm so glad we have all these people helping us, and that a part of me can rescue you."

The signature was blurred.

The last entry was yesterday. In ink. In the book. *Not on some serrated page torn from a notebook.*

"Don't let anything steal your love for God. You are worthy of His love. He still has you engraved on the palms of His hands."

Maia turned the tiny book. In the side margin, a scribbled message—*perhaps an afterthought.* "If I don't make it back home, you know where I'll be. See you there." The signature was barely legible.

Maia folded the serrated note and closed the book. She chewed her lip. *I can't bear to lose Shelby now.*

But the idea of somebody having her engraved on the palms of His hands—*bizarre place for a tattoo.*

Maia threw the book into the plastic bag. *Well, you can forget that! Sounds creepy.*

49

Desai is having another party. This time darker, with more candles, more liquor per cocktail, and the THC and sage already burning.

Maia arrived thirty minutes late. Late enough to make an entrance. She dressed for the event, complete with jeans, ankle boots, and borrowed bling from Tanya.

She removed her mask and scanned the room for that good-looking guy and his muscular roommate from the last party. *Too bad COVID put these boys back home with their mommas. They could be a lot of fun in their own place.*

Desai floated between her guests, the saffron sheers dancing in the spring breeze coming through the window.

"Maia, we're having another Cat Scratch tonight. I put you first on the list."

Maia sat her Coke and rum on the counter. "I just want to know how my dad will die. I figure it's a simple question, right?"

After all, this is not scientific. It's likely a spoof.

Desai shut the window and pulled the burgundy velvets to block the dusk. She lit more candles as the circle gathered.

Maia relaxed her head in Desai's lap, brushing the hair away from her temples. She asked her question.

"Aha! But you are the one I want dead!" the voice cackled.

A cool gust entered the room. The curtains shimmied. *Impossible.* Maia felt the carpet beneath her shirt. Her back was on fire, her shoulders stinging. The floor vibrated. Her head buzzed.

She tried to stand. But the world danced an irregular jig. *No secured carpet. No solid footing.*

Maia reeled against the wall. Her temple splintered. *Deep purple. Beautiful purple. Swirls of black ink.*

Suddenly garish.

"I have been trying to get you for years!" the voice mocked.

Orange and purple balls charging me, aiming for my eyes, slamming my face, pummeling my chest.

"Leukemia, leukemia, just gave you my leukemia," the voice metered in delight.

That singing is off-key. Distraught, jarring. Maia shivered. The watchers hovered closer.

She flailed her arms, striking at the dark presence. Her hand punched the stuffy air. *Can't hit the beast anyhow!*

A foul odor hit her stomach. She wretched.

The acid from her stomach was on her face, her blouse. On the floor. She curled to hide her chest and her stomach, her knees bent. "Look, I only wanted to know how my dad would die," she whimpered.

"Oh, baby," haunted the voice, as if noting her position. "He'll die like everybody else does—of something!"

Maia garnered her energy to seethe. "Like that virus he works with, thinking he's rescuing them?"

"All of life is a virus. If you don't think so, ask a virologist." The voice laughed.

The voice stopped; the haunting was over.

Maia felt her face. *I don't know any more about my dad than when I came.*

She blew on her palm. It returned moist. *I am still breathing.*

Tanya and Desai lifted Maia's head and shoulders, sitting her toward the door. They lifted her shirt, wicking the parts soaked with sweat and acid. Three red marks streaked her right shoulder. They giggled in delight and laid her back.

She drifted. Asleep? A trance? *To think you can be this confused without a hit or even finishing a martini.*

Maybe I'm just sick. Food poisoning or something.

50

Greg opened the passenger door to his truck. Maia grabbed the rail above the door and hoisted herself in. Greg got in on the driver's side and started the vehicle. Maia took a sideways glance at the driver.

Greg looked nonchalantly in the rearview mirror, backed up, and braked. Then swung onto the narrow road.

Maia rolled down the window, enjoying the spring. Cool air tousled her hair, the wind making its own song, limiting conversation.

Greg hit an arm button and rolled up Maia's window. "So what's been bugging you, Sis?"

Maia upturned her chin. "Sis?"

She rearranged her hair into a bun. "Just stress, that's all."

"Stress? Really?" Greg turned the fan to mild air. "Tell me about it."

"Well, I don't suppose my finding work to avoid Lisa's basement qualifies as stress to you, given your being furloughed from your job and sitting home, doing online school with two kids. And a wife in the hospital."

"It's been a bit of a stretch." He adjusted his ample body into the driver's seat and relaxed his hand on the steering wheel. He looked straight ahead at the oncoming traffic. "Is that all?"

"I feel the whole thing is a crap of lies. They told me to get an education so I could get a good job. Well, I'm getting a job, all right! At least two jobs. Just to just pay the bills. Before I get done with my education." Maia tightened her neck muscles, her fingers tapping her jeans.

"Every job application wants to know my race. Like being white is something I wanted. Now, I'm even whiter since my transplant. Supposedly, I'm a person of privilege. As if attending college, working nights, going without sleep, having no money, and the constant threat of living with your mom and stepdad is a privilege. But that's what they claim."

Greg braked for a stop. "How many people in the world—regardless of race—would love to have the privilege of your problems?" Greg started through the intersection. "Do you think the new black and colored privilege is a bit of payback for the old white privilege?"

Maia jutted her chin, peering straight ahead. "I have no idea. But none of this is my fault. I didn't decide to be born white, and my father to be a doctor. I didn't decide to get leukemia and the long-term problems of a transplant."

She paused her finger tapping. Picked a cat hair off her jeans. "Maybe we should all do a DNA test and see how much we really have in common? How about an economics paper detailing how much money people are making just exploiting our differences?"

"How about power? Not money." Greg let up on the gas pedal.

Maia ignored him.

Clicking and blinking from the turn signal.

"They claim this virus came from China, as if anybody can prove that. This virus is said to be affecting people of color worse than others. And men. Sorry," Maia's eyes stared at the speedometer, "but I hate men. They've created much of what's wrong with the world. At least, that's what Mom says."

Greg slowed for the turn. "So that's what Lisa says, huh? Are you certain about that?"

Maia put her hand on the dashboard. "I think it's all just corrupted history. Antiracism is the most wonderfully racist thing I can imagine. Systemic racism is old. Majorities always misuse minorities. None of this is really new, just recycled mental garbage. New meanings to old words. The same old garbage. Intersectionality is just relabeled discrimination. Even obnoxious viruses are nothing new—happened in 1918 and 1957, just to people in their twenties and forties, not the old people."

Greg looked at Maia's hand, stiff on the dashboard. "Does my driving frighten you?"

She returned her hand to her lap. "Sorry. Sometimes I do that when I'm upset."

Greg looked back to the roadway. "It's also nothing new—that most people let other people down." Greg swallowed. "Like your parents disappointed you. Devalued you."

Maia gave him an evil eye. "You have no clue. That's before you and Shelby were even dating. Dad left just before I turned twelve. He just packed up one Christmas and told the family that he was leaving. Moved out and divorced Mom. Mom dissolved a bit and is still not herself. That was the Christmas before I got leukemia, before I lost my hair. I've hated Christmas ever since. It keeps coming every year, though. As if one year, it might get better."

Maia flipped her hair out of its bun. She ran her fingers up her scalp to clench a fist of hair. "This year though, 2020, is the worst!"

Greg pulled into the near-empty clinic parking lot. "Shelby's van is the one in the handicap parking space, second from the door. Looks like the windshield is clear." He managed a kiddish smile. "She doesn't have a ticket. The parking officer must be furloughed too."

Maia chirped, "Since her van is the only car still in the parking lot, it's not hard to find."

"She doesn't have a handicap sticker, you know," Greg joked. Then frowned. "Not yet, anyhow."

Greg helped Maia out of the truck, bumped her elbow as allowed, and handed her the keys to Shelby's van. "See you back in our driveway. Thanks for the company."

He winked. "Sisters always give me a lot to think about."

Maia grunted and clutched the keys.

She opened the van door and glanced to the back. Evidence of kid-life—half-finished beverages with straws sticking out, crumbled sweatshirts, athletic jerseys. Coupons peeking out of a used envelope.

The front still smelled of Shelby's perfume, her abandoned shoes pivoted into the passenger's floor space.

She must have been too swollen to wear them.

51

Jakeem felt a presence. Saw a flicker of light.

His head throbbed. His back burned.

The dragon. *Now lodged in his throat.*

He tried to move his hands. *Banded in place.*

The whiteboard beyond his bed claimed that it had been over fifty days since that white liquid streamed up his vein.

He looked at the ceiling. The ants were gone. *No cockroaches attacking his arms.*

He sensed the presence beside him again. He could barely see a nurse on his right side, hanging a bag of IV fluids.

He squirmed.

She looked his way. Their eyes met.

Victor and cheerleader, meeting near the finish line.

He felt a tear on his cheek. She took a tissue in her gloved hand and wiped it.

He was back. At least partly back.

The respiratory therapist came and removed the tube from the ventilator. She took a measurement, scribbled on her paper, then reattached the tube. More forced breaths. She left.

She was hurrying to the door when he grunted.

He didn't recognize the sound.

He couldn't talk.

But she heard me.

She turned back, still wearing the gown, gloves, and a cap that hid her hair. She had hazel eyes above the mask.

"You have a way to go. But you've made it this far," she offered, uncertainty and hope mixed in her eyes.

A human voice. Another human, another voice.

I didn't die after all.

Jakeem couldn't remember the rolling bed, the ventilator, the tracheostomy, the central lines, the big catheter in his neck. He had no idea how many humans had met his needs, kept him alive, doing their daily jobs in spite of his uncertain prognosis.

Some machine kept coming every day for several hours. It sat and buzzed and acted as if he should know who it was. *I'm not certain I like this.*

The air hissing of that ventilator machine kept him awake at night.

One day, Dr. Ben Lawson came in and announced that the kidney machine wasn't needed anymore. *Can't say I'm sorry to see that thing leave.*

The physical therapist came to exercise his arms and legs. She said tomorrow he would get up to a chair. *Such a deal. A chair. I must be a king to have a chair.*

To be this important.

The respiratory therapist came every eight hours and made the same measurements.

He was thinking more clearly. He could remember names. Missing words suddenly showed up. He started counting to ten in his head. Maybe twenty, maybe thirty. He sang the alphabet song in his brain. *I have to start somewhere. Maybe someday, they'll give me a crossword puzzle.* The thought made him tired.

He dozed.

The nurse said some lady named Cherika called frequently. Jakeem liked this news. *Right much.* But then, he had a long way to go. The breathing lady said so. *Cherika is one fine lady. I know my limits.* He wasn't ready for the likes of her, no matter how much he would like her right now.

The next day, he was in the wheelchair for twenty minutes. It seemed like twenty hours.

He slept the rest of the day.

Dr. Ben came back the following day. He said Jakeem's heart was behaving. The lungs were better. Today they would do a "weaning trial," whatever that is. They detached the tubing to the ventilator and changed the settings. He was on his own. His chest muscles hurt from the effort. He couldn't breathe, his thinking fogged up. The clock on the wall above the foot of the bed said he made it for five minutes.

Hours and days passed. Jakeem lost track of time. He tried to move, to help those trying to lift him in the bed. But he was weak. *Weak as a cat,* Momma would say. He had no idea how weak a cat could be. Seems a mouse could take him on and win about now.

Jakeem dozed between therapies. He had weaning trial after weaning trial. He failed them all.

One day, though, they left him off the ventilator. "Just on the t-piece," they said. For a full thirty minutes. *I think I'm making it.*

One day, Dr. Ben Lawson told him he could get rid of the breathing tube.

Jakeem had adjusted to the dragon.

Fear. Fear of living without the ventilator to breathe.

The next morning, with the first hint of sun over the city, the respiratory therapist came in, awakened Jakeem with the suctioning, deflated the cuff, and replaced the tubing with a small cannula of oxygen.

Jakeem had made it off the vent.

You would have thought I was the mayor of the city! Happy, tear-laden eyes lit up behind the masks. Joyful words came from the mask-hidden mouths of near strangers.

Jakeem had survived to get off the ventilator. His heart was working, his kidneys were improving, and his lungs could hold their own with just nasal oxygen. *Who knows if my brain will clear? Who knows if I will ever work as a CNA again?*

* * *

Dr. Ben Lawson stood in silence at the foot of Jakeem's bed, then walked to the window, looking down. Only a few refrigerator trucks remained, still parked with military precision.

If God is good, and it appears He has been, Jakeem will leave the hospital another way.

52

Dr. Ed Clarke hailed a taxi. To the children's hospital. On the other side of the city.

He had his mask, his plastic face shield, and his ID tag prominently displayed. His polished shoes glistened in the afternoon sun. He wore his suit, fresh from the dry cleaners, with a clean white lab coat folded over his forearm.

Ed stared from the back seat of the taxi, amazed at the lack in the city.

Lack of people, lack of traffic. No garbage pickup. Litter spilling from the alleys. Stores and restaurants shuttered, empty windows staring at the few cars who snuck down the naked avenues.

This dastardly virus has changed everything!

The entry staff took his temperature at the door and asked questions about fever, cough, and any gastrointestinal problems.

He punched the elevator button to the fifth floor, then wandered the lonely halls.

Stale. Silent. A mere whisper echoed like a megaphone.

The ICU used to be over there. Now hollow, silent.

A spattering of office chairs. An unplugged coffee maker. Dry.

The thriving physical therapy clinic—evacuated—a few offices still sporting abandoned cups or a rare computer tablet, still plugged in.

Tables and balls and devices for learning to crawl and tumble and walk. Still in their bins.

Sagging charts for learning to see and earphones for hearing. Lopsided on the walls.

The inner room—where the twins had been—had new walls. A few linens lay scattered about the four-wheeled carts, half pushed in haste. *Perhaps re-designated as a linen closet?*

The tiles on the floor of the closet were the same, though. Tiles of blue, pink, and white flecks. Dr. Ed Clarke blinked.

He found an old tissue in his right pants pocket and lifted his mask to blow his nose.

The elevator door opened and closed.

No footsteps followed the closing of the elevator. The sound faded.

A vacant place? Alone?

The air smelled musty.

"Can I ever reverse this?"

Dr. Ed Clarke knelt on the dusty, cold tiles. He flipped his name tag and closed the doors behind him.

If only I could be forgiven?

If only I could change some things. I am still trying to get Steven back into the canoe, to do that day over again.

I can smell the grass, the dew; my ears hear the jokes and the paddles dipping the water. Laughing that we only had two life jackets for three people and Steven didn't have one on. Can't find the part of my brain where Steven fell into the water—flailing and screaming. The canoe capsizing as we tried to rescue him. The seconds of silence when Steven went under the water for the last time.

Nausea. The rescuers arriving, the questions, the funeral. Dad and Mom drenched over the coffin. The cold breeze as we all left the cemetery.

Ed had never gone back. He had run forever—to track meets, to scholarships, to college, to excellence, to medical school, to marriage, to kids, to divorce. Hoping to find relief from a deep pain, a memory stuffed so far down. A buried grief that mourned, that soured every waking moment.

I hoped if I did everything right, I might be forgiven.

And then the twins happened.

Does God really have the last vendetta? The last poke at my fragile self?

"These decisions are legal now. Why doesn't my gut feel any better?"

Endless nights of pondering, hoping to dream a different ending to this nightmare. *I wonder if my dying patients have more peace than I do.*

His demons rose to torture him. *Is God really so good? Or is God just out to get you? A vindictive God, looking to punish you for every mistake? Or is your brain just believing lies? Are your memories even accurate, anyhow? Are your memories just neurons firing to torture you?*

Neglected people flitted through his mind. *Shelby, Maia, Dana. Even Lisa. This had never been fair to her. She had gone from being a competent mother to a broken woman who smoked weed as her major pastime.*

She likely wants to forget as much as I do.

"If only I could be forgiven. If only my past would not excoriate me forever."

He had forgotten how to pray.

But God did not forget.

God sent His one and only Son to die.

That Jesus I have hated and essentially spat on in the past?

He is still waiting?

For me?

A creation. Lost. But still a created person.

"Dear Jesus, I am so sorry—I can never make this right. I am so, so sorry."

Gritty knees and aching thighs.

Years and years of regret.

Wet splotches on a starched shirt.

Torment hissed. Then evaporated.

Steven appeared. He was older, fresh-shaven, smiling. He was not angry.

Ed's tears washed the tiny faces. The blue eyes and blonde curls were angels with kind smiles. They were older, separate, holding hands. No scars, normal hair. He could see love in their eyes.

They were smiling. Unoffended.

Ed found a clean handkerchief in his left pants pocket. He blew his nose.

The sun was setting. The front of his shirt was getting cold. It was still moist, his name tag still backward.

Ed stood. Taller than before.

He dusted his knees and the toes of his shoes.

God had forgiven him. He had forgiven God.

Lisa might never forgive him. *Understandable.*

Ed Clarke had started to forgive Ed Clarke.

Dr. Clarke turned his name tag to its proper reading. He gently closed the doors to the linen closet.

The walls of this place are monuments to mercy, to a God who loves us in our failures.

The doorknobs reflected an incredulous face.

No one else might ever know, but this unmarked linen closet is an Ebenezer.

Undeserved.

53

Another call. Familiar prefix, unfamiliar last seven numbers. Dr. Ben hit the button on his phone.

The fragile female voice on the other end wanted to be certain she was talking to a "Dr. Ben Lawson."

She stammered, as if intimidated to be talking to such an important person. Someone at her church thought he would want to know—that a child, a girl related to his patient named Zapota, had been found at a nearby feeding program. Church members, working with social services, were matching the child with a Spanish-English family.

Yes, this elderly lady was still helping the girl with remote school, using a computer. And this girl was the same age as her own granddaughter, isolated out of state during the pandemic.

"I asked God to let me be of use during this pandemic. He answered my prayers." She sniffled and chuckled in the same sentence. "I'm an old lady, you know."

Dr. Ben grabbed his pen from his pocket and fumbled for his clipboard.

"Is that all?"

"No, I don't need anything else." She paused before she said goodbye. "I just wanted 'a Dr. Ben' to know. That's all."

* * *

Dr. Ben was scrubbed in a procedure in the ICU. He missed the phone call.

Laura left a message. She and the kids were coming home soon. The weather was getting hotter in Florida. Maybe the politicians would open the city from the COVID lockdown by July. She hoped to bring the kids home the next allowed weekend that Ben was off call.

Ben reviewed the calendar on his phone. *This is Sunday, May 10. Mother's Day.*

The fight was not over.

But Laura was calling a truce.

54

Ben needed some advice about Laura. *There's a rectory within a few blocks. My next afternoon away from the hospital.*

The faded stone building shadowed its latticed windows from the afternoon sun. Dr. Ben Lawson stood beneath the arched alcove and slipped a medical journal beneath his lab coat. He stepped backward, barely missing a pool of water at the head of the sidewalk.

He rang the doorbell again.

Father Tournier put down his calligraphy nib and arranged the linen papers to dry. He put on his mask and stodged his ample frame to open the door, his face red and scaling with his age, his hair slicked back. Fiery eyes hid behind his plastic frames.

He lifted his chin to peer at Dr. Ben's name tag. "I see you're a man of the stethoscope."

Ben squinted to see the eyes behind scratches in the old man's lenses. "And you're a man of the cloth."

This repository of ancient knowledge motioned Ben inside and closed the door.

"What brings you here so late today?" The priest's cane tapped a slow cadence down the hall. *Galoshes on the rubber mat, coat hung on the metal rung above.*

Dr. Ben followed the cane's pointing to the center of the room, to the one chair across from a heavy oak desk. *Odd place. Hopefully not symbolic.*

"I'm here for two things. I'm here for help with my marriage." Ben sat straight-backed, pen and legal pad in hand. "And I'd also like to know if the church has changed its position on suicide." Ben cleared his throat. "I suppose you read about the doctor who killed himself. Seems this COVID finished him before we knew if he had the virus."

The priest toddled to the couch, tossed the pillows, and plopped into its mold.

"They're not the only ones dying, from what I hear."

"Yes, two other doctors, father and son, have died of this blasted disease. They caught the virus, likely from a patient they were treating. But this guy just shot himself. Bad for his kids, I think."

The priest eyed his end table and toggled a small bell. "Worse for his soul."

"How much worse for his soul?" Ben turned his chair to face the couch.

"Seems one should be strong of soul." The priest exhaled. "With all that dying, one should be closer to the afterlife than to earth." He ran two fingers around his neck, adjusting his clerical collar. "Was his soul already gone before this virus ever landed here?"

Father Tournier motioned his rectory assistant to pour Ben some tea. He poured himself a shot of Jameson Irish.

"Maybe the electronic health record, the hassle of administrators and government intrusions, had already eroded his soul."

"Is that all?"

Dr. Ben sat forward. "Electronic medical records make keyboarding and data entry seem like high school. Trivial. It takes time away from patients, away from kids and family. It's the new variation of long-call. 'Pajama time at home,' doing charts until the wee hours while the kids sleep and the spouse tosses."

"Is the computer the real problem? Or just a symptom of the problem?" The priest adjusted his position on the couch to face Ben. "Why don't you hire a scribe? Take some computer courses? Set up templates to make you faster at completing notes?"

"Well, it's not just the computerized records." Dr. Ben shifted back in the chair. "Many medical people suffer from being forced to watch, and vicariously condone, procedures and decisions which violate their consciences. Sometimes these are even medically counter-intuitive."

"Do you think that's really all there is? To the problems medical people have?"

Dr. Ben looked at the floor. "We should have been prepared for a pandemic. For God's sake, we put a man on the moon. But we only have N95 masks—with their oversized pores—to protect us from viruses?" The chair squeaked. "We trusted our outsourcing, thinking this was just another new startup. I guess we didn't see the downsides of our decisions."

"You didn't realize that this was an international war of ideologies?" the priest questioned.

Ben peered at the priest. "It's deeper than that. I've lied to the very people I took an oath to protect."

"Lied about what?" Father T took a first sip.

"Lied about tests the patient wanted but I declined. Lied about the day they needed to head home, because I felt pressured by the discharge planner. I didn't want to tell the patient that the census required a new patient for the bed, that hospital administration was watching my performance and sending me notices if I adversely affected the bottom line. This was before the pandemic, I need to add. Who knows what will happen next?"

Father T took another sip. "Sounds like you have an ideological war in medicine too."

Ben twisted on the chair.

The priest gazed at the window. "Do you think this is really that different, say, from the time of Hippocrates? As our culture changes, is Hippocrates even important anymore?"

"Well, Hippocrates must have known more about humans than we do."

"Hippocrates was pre-Christian by more than 300 years. But Hippocrates didn't believe in abortion or infanticide. Did he know something that we don't?"

The priest repositioned his feet in front of the couch.

"And the Greeks accepted homosexual relations but reserved marriage as a structure of the state, for the future of citizens and the republic. Have we evolved beyond them?"

"I heard the early Christians started rescuing babies from the hillsides, then started hospitals for the poor," Ben offered.

"Oh, really? That was during Roman times. After the Greeks." Father T started folding the couch shawl beside him. "Does your current hospital look like it would rescue anybody from a hillside?"

Ben raised his voice. "We're beyond that now. We have science. And we're rescuing immigrants from the projects, putting them on ventilators, giving them expensive medications. Knowing they can't, and never will be able to, pay for them."

Ben sat up straight, the wheels of his chair groaning his interjection. "Respectfully, Father, I didn't come here for a long discussion. I need something to help me today. I don't care about the Greeks, and I don't care about the Romans or the Christians. We're in the age of science. New things are coming. I'm sure we'll figure COVID out soon. We have virologists and vaccines on the way."

"Good. Then I have a question." The priest leaned forward, his forehead creased above his mask. "If we worry about overpopulation, and old people have outdated beliefs, why are they scheduled to get any vaccines first? Why would a few thousand deaths matter? If you believe in survival of the fittest, and there are over eight billion people on Earth, why would you spend precious resources to save the pitiful few that are only going to die in the next ten years anyhow? Why not spend those resources on the healthy who have a chance to survive? Those who might thrive in the new climate change?"

"I'm uncertain if politicians know much about STEM subjects," Ben breathed.

"Don't blame the politicians. I'm just asking why are we trying to save the old, the infirm? One could infer that the old have outdated ideas, can't use computers well. The infirm take from society and contribute little. Seems that the sooner they die off, the quicker the new world can become a reality. Survival of the fittest, you know."

Ben crossed his feet. "Maybe that shouldn't apply to Grandma."

Father T tossed the shawl on top of the pillows. "Maybe Darwin should be taken in the context he deserves. Darwin published extrapolations from observations. Observational science.

"No randomized controlled populations, no evidence-based studies—as are currently expected. Maybe an uncritical devotion to Darwin's hypothesis is religion, not true science?" The priest leaned forward and whispered into his mask. "Is it possible that what is now called 'science' is just political science?"

The priest let out a long sigh and gazed at the ceiling. "Maybe our society is just more into technology than it is into science. More into convenience than curiosity. Maybe our technology has outdistanced our wisdom. Just because something CAN be done, that it SHOULD be done--what used to be called the *technological imperative*?"

Father T twisted off his glasses and fumbled a handkerchief from his frock, then wiped sweat from his face. "Why else do you think we have CRISPR twins? Engineered to resist HIV, a disease they may never encounter?" The old man chuckled. "Maybe we should engineer a baby resistant to COVID-19?"

Ben glimpsed the time on his phone. *Why are we discussing CRISPR babies? After all, they were engineered in a petri dish, then born in China last year—before the pandemic. I didn't come here for a history lesson or an intellectual discussion.*

Father T peered at Ben again, his eyebrows raised. "You're young. What else do you think this 'cancel culture' has truncated? How many other ideas do you have that fit reality better than what you've learned in establishment education? In medicine?"

Ben scraped his feet, hearing the grit of dirt on the wooden floor.

Father T's eyes did not follow the scrape. "Cancel culture came from the therapist's office, telling troubled kids they didn't have to think or talk about anything that upset them. An immature way to deal with problems. Just shut it out. Hope it will go away. Keeps people trapped. Perpetual income for the therapist, though."

The priest continued the mutter into his mask. "And you wonder why the public doesn't trust you to tell them the truth?" His eyes narrowed. "Maybe you haven't reviewed the actual data? Maybe you don't even know the truth yourself?"

Ben sighed. *Enough guilt for the day. I've been in the hospital for weeks with COVID patients. Laura is coming home. I need to get some guidance about Laura.*

Ben cleared his throat. "I need to discuss the basics."

Father T took the last swig of the shot of whiskey.

"Okay. Back to your questions about the church's stance on suicide and marriage."

The eyes behind the scratched lenses seemed suddenly sad.

"Maybe that doctor deserves mercy for ending his own suffering. I used to see people like him in confession every day, before COVID kept everybody home. People in pain, no hope, feeling lost."

Ben sighed and rubbed his eyes. He staggered to stand.

"Father," he inserted, "I think the isolation with COVID has made you think too much. What I came here for—what I came here for, was not a discussion of the philosophies of medicine or science. I need help with my marriage."

"Start with definitions," the priest rebounded, still planted on the couch. "Tell me how you define marriage, and I'll tell you what your problem is."

"Marriage is. . ." Ben paused and shifted back to the chair. "Marriage is two people committing to each other for the sake of the future, to care for each other in sickness and in health, forsaking all others, until death do you part."

"Glad to see that you remember part of what you promised that day." Father T placed his glass on the side table. "Why only two?"

"Well, human nature being what it is. Two is about the maximum one could expect to keep such a promise."

"And tell me what you know about human nature?" Father T struggled out of the couch and tottered across the room.

Ben's eyes followed him. "Well, humans are reportedly fickle, weak, and cowardly; if we like what we see, we take it. We hate discomfort. We hate being told *no*. So we don't keep promises very well. And most of the time, we aren't very kind."

The priest started opening drawers, shuffling papers. "Does a wonderful education make good people?" He slammed a drawer. "Who constructs the definition of good? What if the definition of *good* changes?"

The priest stood, hands on hips, his frock shorter. "Who helps such humans keep their promises? Who is responsible? The individual, genetics, or society?"

He bent to rummage through more drawers. "Perhaps I should preface. Those promises aren't very reliable. I preside over lots of marriages, see lots of divorced people. Have you ever heard the word *covenant*?"

"*Covenant*—well, I haven't heard that word since catechism. Correct that." Ben rubbed his palm. "Maybe at our wedding."

The priest arranged the linen sheets in front of him on the empty desktop. "A covenant is a human-deity connection, more than a contract, more than a promise."

Father T plunked in a complaining chair and picked up his pen. "And some Jews and some Christians think God keeps his half of the agreement even when the human part chickens out."

Father T positioned the nib. "And marriage is a covenant."

Dr. Ben scowled. "So that means that even though humans give up, get divorced, have kids, and don't parent them, that God just keeps on doing His part." Ben hid a smirk behind his mask. "You realize that most of society thinks this opinion is something to be avoided in a cow pasture."

The priest tilted his pen again and straightened his back to the calligraphy angle. "Well, it makes God's job a lot harder when humans shirk."

Father T crafted three letters in silence. A hint of sunlight drifted through the window, dust dancing like old glitter.

Ben looked toward the door.

"Say, Ben, why did you go into medicine in the first place?" The priest stared at the letters on the page, fanning them to dry. "Did you really think little you could make a difference in the big universe that is God's?"

The clock ticked on the wall. Shadows slid through the window. Noises like a late garbage collector banging bins in the alley.

"Do you think God gave you Laura as a helpmate to make you the best doctor in the world? Did God really think you had such great potential that He had to give you a woman of such quality in order to achieve all He had planned? Do you think you really warranted such a jewel of a lady?"

Ben looked at the clock, then at the drying letters. Still moist.

Father T looked up. "Have you ever thanked God for Laura, that He allowed you and not some other, more impressive guy to be her husband? Did you ever consider this?"

Ben pressed his lips. His eyes looked for a nearer exit.

"Do you think marriage is some construct to have free sex and legal heirs? Now, even gay couples have this right. The Greeks didn't have this, but the USA and most of Europe does.

"Forget marriage. What about medicine? Only a few doctors take the Hippocratic oath; the rest say something else. Did they stand before God and their families and make promises? To protect their patients? In Hippocratic cases, to not prescribe deadly potions or abortifacients? You realize that the proscription against abortion came 300 years before Jesus Christ? Did your medical classmates really say these things or just mumble them in the auditorium's dark, knowing all the while they would never keep, or had already broken, such oaths? Do such doctors know that they've already started the slide to moral violation, the path to the suicide of their souls?"

Father T held up the linen page. Still sheen on the letters.

"How is making promises in medicine any different from standing before a candlelit altar or a family shrine and promising to care long term for one other person?" He bent to open a lower drawer. "Or maybe they promised nothing. They just expected to be happy as long as the benefit to themselves lasted. In short, their promise is as good as their convenience."

Ben scanned his white knuckles and rolled the platinum band on his left fourth finger.

"You realize, Father," Ben cautioned to insert, "that a significant percentage of doctors don't take the Hippocratic oath now because they come from other traditions, many non-Western, and study medicine for many reasons. They're good people, caring doctors, and brilliant scientists, but they don't share your belief system. For them, pursuing medicine is an honor to their family or a secular career requiring brilliance."

The priest adjusted his feet beneath the desk. "But you are here. Which implies that you do share my belief system. You are worried about your covenant marriage and you believe a physician should be honest to God's creatures and care for them as responsibly as possible."

Father T adjusted a new linen and tilted his pen again. "Perhaps you need to rethink your definition of marriage and your mandate to medicine. If you start with the basics, you'll know how to change your behavior."

The priest stared at the linen sheet, his forehead wrinkled. "I could give you lists, but the best lists will spring from your soul, once your spirit is straight."

The rotary desk chair groaned as the priest moved it aside. "And you still have a soul." The priest headed to the door. "You have a spirit, which knows God, and which knows that something is wrong in your world. You also have a thinking mind within your soul that understands that suicide is not the way out. Whether it's a mortal sin, you and the Church may disagree."

The priest paused, a hand on the doorknob. "But suicide is a deadly and permanent solution to an otherwise temporary situation. It begets only more problems—for you and for your progeny."

Ben stood, partly smiled, and tilted a nod. The door squeaked open.

Ben whisked outside, shrugging to hide a gulp of fresh air. A breeze hid the mutter beneath his mask: No *"to-do list."* Nothing to show for the two hours spent in this stale rectory. Two hours spent with this smug old man and his dinosaur ways of thinking.

Father T opened the door wider to yell at Ben's figure swallowing in the dusk. "You are too smart and too courageous to give up now."

Dr. Ben Lawson heard a powerful stride on the pavement. *I might have to bow and twist, but I will lick this python after all.*

55

Dr. Ben's footsteps echoed in the linoleum hall. He licked his dry lips. *I don't recall Dr. Clarke's office being so far from the doctors' lounge.*

He stared at the plaque beside the door:

Edward M. Clarke, M.D., PhD
Professor of Medicine
Division Pulmonary and Intensive Care

He turned the doorknob to Dr. Clarke's office and caught his balance. *Heavy door.*

"Come in." The back of Dr. Clarke's head remained fixed, a blue screen in front of him.

Dr. Ben stood for several seconds.

"What do you want?" Dr. Clarke finally spoke to the presence behind him.

"More time off," Dr. Lawson blurted.

Dr. Clarke spun around in his chair, his jaw jutting forward. The lines in his face hardened.

Dr. Ben took a deep breath. "I need more time away from this place. If I don't get some priorities straight,

I'm going to lose everything I've worked for. I'm going to lose my marriage and my family. And my sanity. I didn't pursue medicine to become famous. I did it to become a real physician."

Dr. Clarke dropped his eyes. "You are wiser than I thought."

Dr. Ben stood.

Silence.

Noise in the hall. Dr. Clarke twisted back to his desk and picked up a pen. "I'll check with the team and the scheduler. Who knows when this pandemic will end? Who knows when the mayor and the governor will lighten the restrictions?" He sighed. "But help has arrived for now, at least."

Dr. Clarke scribbled on a notepad.

He clicked on his keyboard.

Silence.

The wheels on Dr. Clarke's chair squeaked. "Seems you're not the only doctor who wants some time to regroup. I'll let you know in six weeks, when the new schedule comes out."

Dr. Ben took a shallow breath and moved toward the door.

The hall no longer echoed.

He licked his cracked lips.

56

Maia sat down for her morning cup of coffee. She punched Dana's number. "Do you have anything planned for Memorial Day?"

"Jeremy and I are staying in the basement." Dana turned down his music. "The newscasters seem worried because lots of people are heading to the beaches and social distancing may be compromised, especially at a beach. They said the president canceled his trip to Brazil—there are a lot of COVID cases reported there."

"Well, people can still wear their masks at the beach," Maia asserted. "And the president is speaking at Arlington today, so the restrictions must be easing some." Maia finished her bite of guacamole toast and took a sip of coffee. "Have you heard any more about your surgery? Have they rescheduled it yet?"

"Haven't heard anything." Dana coughed into the phone. "But remind Tanya that her 'essential' clinic will be open tomorrow. They've had no scheduling interruptions the whole pandemic."

"Why are you intruding into such a private issue? After all, this doesn't involve you." Maia took a sip. "By the way, have you called the sperm clinic yet? After all, your surgery won't be postponed forever."

"Don't you think you're being racist—reminding me to freeze some semen at the sperm clinic? You're acting like my DNA is better than hers." Dana turned up his music. "My sister is being a hypocrite," he warbled.

"The decision is not up to me. It's her body, her choice."

Maia punched out of the call.

57

Tanya shuffled out of the bedroom. "I think I'm ready."

"Ready for what?"

"To end this pregnancy and get this behind me. Jethro has a new woman."

"Have you called the clinic?"

"Yes, I've already called. Have an appointment for tomorrow morning. Started pills yesterday to soften things down there a bit. But I don't want this kid to hear about it. They start hearing about the fifth month, don't they?"

"You spend too much time on the computer studying fetal development."

Tanya opened the refrigerator.

"Just want to be informed. By the way, I'll need a driver."

* * *

Tanya awakened to her baby kicking, her abdomen jiggling. "Hey, little one, it's the middle of the night." Tanya rolled onto her side. "I shouldn't call you *little one*—after all, you're only a clump of cells. I just waited too long, that's all."

Her hand went to her belly. "Little one, I don't want you growing up without a daddy. He doesn't want you. Daddy has a new woman in another state. But he's coming back into town. He may want Momma again. You know, to be his woman."

The ambient light from the town snuck across her tummy: "Your kicks started like butterflies in the belly. Last week I could see you stirring. But no pokes yet. No rolling waves in my belly like they talk about."

Tanya got up to the bathroom, rearranged her pillow, and adjusted the blankets. "As they say, you'll never have to be black in America, little one." She patted her belly as she drifted into sleep. "Maybe I'll see you in Heaven if that's where you go."

***

The alarm blared. Tanya bopped it on the sixth bleep.

"Today is the day."

She packed the jeans that she had worn on New Year's Eve. "They were a little snug then. But they'll fit again tonight."

58

Maia started the jeep at 7:10 a.m. and honked once. Tanya walked outside and climbed in.

Neither spoke on the drive to the clinic.

Gray overhead, the morning sun hid behind the clouds, leaving a musty yellow sunrise. Green grass outlined the streets, damp from the recent rain.

Tanya opened the car door, adjusted her mask, and stepped out. She walked to the building alone. *Empty sidewalks. No protestors today.*

The door to the place finally budged. Tanya signed in using a friend's name. *No one will ever know.*

"Except God." Her grandmother's voice came from a hidden speaker. "And you."

Tanya looked around. Only three other women, wearing the mandated masks, were in the waiting room. *No one will ever know.* Tanya surveyed the masked receptionist through the plexiglass barrier.

"Except Maia. She drove you here." The voice on the speaker again.

"Is there something wrong with your speaker?" Tanya questioned the receptionist.

The receptionist pushed a consent for treatment through a slot under the window. "Be certain to sign the other consent for an antifertility insert in the arm." She peered at Tanya over her mask. "I assume you don't want to do this again."

"Well, Medicaid is paying for it. They paid for my prenatal care."

"Did you remember to bring your Medicaid card with you?"

"No, I left it at home."

"Well, cash or a credit card will do." The receptionist pointed to the card reader outside the plexiglass. "The machine to your left will process your transaction."

Tanya fumbled through her purse. She counted the bills, came up short. She fumbled again, found her credit card.

* * *

"Right this way." The receptionist ushered her beyond the gray door. "The procedure will be over in no time."

A masked nurse appeared with an IV kit. "This won't feel much different than a pap smear. Just put your legs up in these stirrups."

Tanya put her feet into the cold stirrups. She bent toward her once-purple toenails. "I need to get a pedicure with some new nail polish. Black or a deeper blue this time." She chuckled to the nurse.

The nurse bustled her IV tote into place and thumped Tanya's arm. "Just a little stick, some medicine for pain, and the doctor will be in."

"Who's doing my procedure?"

"Well, let's see." The nurse turned to face a paper on the wall. "The doctors rotate."

"I just wanted to know." Tanya stared at the consent forms. She wiped a tear with her hand, then stiffened her shoulders. She whispered to the ceiling, "Now or never. No diapers for me."

"Oh, it's Dr. Jones today. But it doesn't really matter who does the procedure. You won't remember it, anyway. It'll be over in thirty minutes, and you'll be on your way in an hour."

"I thought she was a psychiatrist."

"Well, it doesn't take much training to do this. Nurses, or even concerned persons can do a menstrual extraction. Dr. Jones rotated through OB-GYN during medical school, you know."

"But I'm a little further along. Like five or six months."

"It's no problem. I'm sure the doctor can handle it."

"Will they pay for this insert in my arm too?"

"Yep, all covered. It was included in your payment when you signed in."

Tanya scribbled the name of a friend across the bottom of the consent form. Medication was already marching up the IV tubing. She was so sleepy.

Her eyelids closed.

* * *

A mask hid the doctor's face. She did not glance at the patient. She gloved up, lubed up, and examined the pelvis.

The quick ultrasound showed twenty-five weeks gestational age. "But on the small side."

Dr. Jones inspected the surgical tray: speculum, catheter, instruments. The suction machine gurgled from the wall. The doctor opened the cervix.

"Don't you try to swim away from me, you little beast," the doctor mumbled.

The nurse shifted uncertain eyes above her mask. She folded her gloved hands at her waist and looked at the instrument tray.

The tenaculum found the feet. "Turn around here," the doctor directed the fetus.

One swift twirl and the head was down, the feet up. Tenaculum out. Head out. The doctor took a quick look at the vocal cords and cut them. "No more crying over this one."

The suction machine hissed out amniotic fluid. "Nice try." The fluid wave on the ultrasound was almost gone.

A vessel pumped blood from the torn cervix.

"Larger scissors."

It took at least four swipes to sever the head.

"Fetal brain coming your way." The doctor muttered to the nurse, who produced a pan of dry ice.

The nurse put the specimen in the box addressed to a university neurology research department. "You'll need to call the courier. Fresh specimen on its way."

Next, one arm torn and delivered. Then the other torn and delivered. Finally, the thighs and feet.

"Don't crush the pelvis. Fetal ovaries. They'll want those," the doctor reminded.

"Placenta delivered."

The doctor rested her gloved hands on her surgical gown. "One less female populating the planet."

She turned to the nurse. "Count the parts before we package and send them. Be certain we got them all."

The nurse placed the pan and the remnants in the body's order. "All parts here. A few fragments left for the blender." The doctor held her gloved hands above her gown, sidestepping blood on the floor, approaching the specimen table.

The doctor picked up a tenaculum and wiggled one leg. "Just look at those thighs!" She turned away. "No marathons for you, honey."

The doctor stepped back to Tanya, still anesthetized, feet still in the stirrups; the doctor reentered the vagina to tamponade the uterus. "Need some suture here for the cervical bleeder."

The nurse scurried to get the suture. The doctor sewed the loop.

Tanya stirred. The nurse flushed more sedative through the IV.

"All done." The doctor flung the gloves while tearing off the gown. "What room do I do next?" She glanced at the nurse. "We need eight of these per day to pay the clinic overhead."

An assistant removed Tanya's feet from the stirrups, covered her with a warm blanket, and transferred her to the recovery area.

Tanya moaned. She grabbed her abdomen.

"Oh, little one," she whimpered.

She sat up abruptly and stared. "It's empty."

She flopped back to the gurney, groping her face. "You're gone."

Tanya smothered the pillow around her head and moaned through her toes.

The nurse held a syringe up to the light, flushed out the air and jabbed the IV port. "Side effect of anesthesia. You'll feel fine as soon as this wears off."

59

The nurse signaled Maia to put on her mask and to pull the car to the exit. Maia helped Tanya into the seat.

Tanya slept the entire route home. Maia helped her hobble to bed.

Tanya slept for three hours. She groaned awake at 2 p.m. *My pad is soaked. The bed is soaked.* She thrust her left forearm above her head. Hidden sutures marked the red injection site. Her right hand massaged her lower belly. She stumbled to the bathroom.

Another pad? *Will this bleeding ever stop? Hints of tissue?*

Maia heard the stirring. She ran to the bathroom where Tanya hovered over the sink. "Is this dizziness normal?" Blood streaked down Tanya's legs.

"What's 'normal' about this, anyhow?" Maia raced to find some towels. "How would I know?"

Blood pooled beyond the towels. Maia pulled a blanket from the closet.

A pool of blood circled beyond the blanket.

"Just lie down and rest." Maia ordered, grabbing two pillows and hoisting Tanya's feet onto them.

"Is this all there is to this?" Tanya whispered to the linoleum tiles. "Is this supposed to end this way?"

Tanya's lips became dry, pale.

Maia bent to drape Tanya's arm to lift her. "Can you help me get you off the floor and into the bed?" Tanya's eyes rolled back.

Maia tugged at her face. Tanya only moaned.

***

Maia punched the emergency button on her phone.

"Yes, my friend just had a procedure, and she's bleeding. And she's no longer talking to me. Can you send someone right away?"

"Stay on the line."

Maia tried to balance the phone while she slid Tanya onto the bed.

Sirens coming this way. Now lights flashing out the window. *Tanya is still not talking to me. But she has a pulse.*

Two masked people put oxygen on Tanya, strapped her onto the gurney, and loaded her into the waiting ambulance. They covered her with blankets, slammed the rear door and restarted the sirens at the end of the driveway.

Maia jumped in her jeep. Ran three red lights, trailing the screaming ambulance to the ER.

Maia slapped a cloth mask over her face at the ER window, hanging on to the ledge. "No, please don't call her family. She's an adult. She wouldn't want that," Maia whispered.

"Well, can you sign for evaluation and treatment?"

"Well, I'm not sure it's legal. She's my roommate. I'm not her guardian."

"Doesn't matter. This is an emergency."

"Paging OB-GYN," the overhead blurted.

"No need to advertise our being here," Maia cautioned, rotating the pen between her pale fingers.

* * *

"Something besides COVID," the paramedic sided to his partner as they raced out the door. Ambulance sirens trailed again into the evening.

Maia sidled along the gurney. "Tanya." She massaged Tanya's pale cheek. No response.

Maia adjusted Tanya's mask. The monitor overhead traced a fast but regular heartbeat.

Maia reached for Tanya's wrist. The pulse was present, but thready and faint.

A lab technician strode into the room, a mask hiding her lower face. "COVID test negative for this patient. I told the designated nurse." She left.

Another nurse whisked into the room.

"Your friend needs an emergency evaluation in the surgery suite. We'll be moving her shortly. I need you to sign a consent, if possible."

"I'm not her legal guardian. I'm just her roommate."

"Well, if you want to save her life, you'll sign."

Maia grabbed the pen and scribbled her name. The nurse paused. "Is this lady under the care of a physician? Do you know if she has taken any medications, including any ordered online?"

"No, I don't think so."

"Does she have any discharge papers from the clinic with the name of the abortion provider?"

Maia shook her head. The nurse grabbed the clipboard and vanished.

Masked orderlies hastened through the door to whisk Tanya down the hall.

Maia stared at the hall, then back to the room, still human hot but empty. "Beautiful Tanya. Maybe I should have tried to stop her from this elective procedure. Seems against nature somehow."

Maia patted the phone in her pocket. She crossed the room and sat down in a darkened corner. "But this is safe, legal, and rare."

She gazed at the large-screen TV, which covered a complete wall. Announcers fixated on the virus. News 24/7. Another newscaster predicting doom, another new plan the government is proposing. Tonight's interview is with a "pajama class" celebrity complaining about the delivery service to their mansion.

She looked at the lamp table. No outdated magazines allowed, either. *COVID takes all.*

The designated nurse flurried up the hall.

"You'll need to leave and wait in your car. Restrictions, you know." The nurse waved Maia to the door. "I'm surprised they let you in. Only one family member allowed for dying patients only."

Maia dodged the water puddles to the jeep and took off her jacket and mask. She turned on the heat and watched the windshield grow fog. Her phone pinged.

* * *

"Did you see the latest posting?"

"No, I haven't seen it yet."

"Yeah, the girl who posted online last night is only seventeen. Sounds pretty courageous to me," Dana chirped.

"What did it show? I'm busy right now."

"Well, it showed several minutes of a white policeman with his knee on a black man's neck. The crowd around screamed for the policeman to get his knee off the man's neck. The man on the ground gasped that he was short of air," Dana puffed. "After the ambulance came, the victim died on the way to the hospital. The news claims an autopsy is pending."

"Were the officers arrested?"

"Yeah. About time somebody did something about this. There were protests starting last night, continuing today. Another one is planned for this evening. By the way, they postponed my surgery again because of COVID. I'm heading out."

"Are you wearing a mask?"

"Doesn't matter. Some wear them, some don't. Racism is worse than this virus."

"But I thought we were supposed to social distance."

"Who cares? This is an issue of social justice."

"Dana. You've been cooped up too long. You've spent too much time in the basement."

"Fresh air and a cause sound good to me. I need something to believe in—for a change."

"What about Jeremy? And Mom?"

"Jeremy is coming too."

"Do you think that video shows the whole story?"

"Well, it shows the part that we need. I can finally be the activist my second-grade teacher wanted!"

"Wait a minute, Dana. I thought people in this country had a right to be presumed innocent until proven guilty. I think we should wait for the cam video and a trial before we pass judgment."

"Well, it's pretty obvious who's guilty here. You're just defending the system," Dana touted. "I'm surprised you're such a white supremacist, a police advocate. You must not have learned much at that college you go to."

"Can't help my intrinsic bias. Everybody has it." Maia quieted. "Well, the system was working for you, until this virus."

"It'll work for me again. Just you wait and see."

60

"I'm calling about my friend who came to the Emergency Room late yesterday. Can you tell me how she is? Is she okay?"

"And your name is?"

"Maia Clarke."

"The computer shows that you are not listed as an approved contact. HIPAA, you know."

"Yeah, I know all about HIPAA. My dad's a doctor at a facility in your network, for God's sake."

"You're not on her list of approved contacts. As you know, I can't give you any information."

"Can't you at least tell me if she's okay? I was with her during this whole thing. I signed for her in the emergency room. I even signed for her surgery."

"Your name is not on her list of approved contacts," the receptionist repeated. "I can't give you any information."

"Did she survive surgery? Is she still in the hospital?"

"I can't tell you if she is here or not. You are not on her list of approved contacts."

Maia tapped the cell button. She interrupted her arm in mid-throw. *Pitching the idiot phone won't solve the problem. I'll try again tomorrow.*

* * *

Tomorrow. Three times.

The next day, four times.

The day following the next day, three times.

Maia sat at the dining table in the early dusk, massaging her temples.

She got up and went into Tanya's bedroom. Cleaned up more blood. *Missed those spatters on the door.*

Tossed the bed covers.

A cell phone—a new one—fell out of the pillowcase. Pictures of persons that resemble Tanya, next to phone numbers.

Maia added the names and numbers to her phone contact list. She looked at the digital clock, then punched the number she hoped belonged to a sister.

"Yes, this is Maia, her roommate. I'm looking for Tanya."

"Yes, she's here. She's right here on the couch, isn't she?" Raucous laughter in the background.

"I was just concerned about her. That's all."

"Oh, she's fine. Got out of the hospital two days ago. Called us to come get her." Throat clearing. "Tanya said we understand her better. She wanted to come home to be with us."

"How should I get her things to you?"

"We're planning to bring her Medicaid card to the financial people at the hospital late Tuesday afternoon. You can leave her things with them."

The line buzzed.

Maia's hand clamped around the cell phone.

Razor blades beckoned loudly from her dresser drawer. *Use me. You'll feel again. Maybe even feel better.*

She dried her face with a non-bloody towel still at the base of the bed.

Maia started to her bedroom, passing the hallway mirror. A blank, stony face—with red eyes and smudged eyeliner—stared back at her.

Maia took a deep breath and exhaled. She brushed the cheap mascara from her cheeks. *I don't have to cut in order to feel.*

She walked to her dresser and opened the hidden place.

Tossed the razor blades into the trash.

61

Maia drove to the hospital late Tuesday morning to deposit Tanya's things with Security.

For a little extra. *Odd request. But a lot of odd things are happening these days. With this virus.*

Dr. Ed Clarke watched the sidewalk and the parking lot from his mid-morning trip to the sixth floor.

Maia headed to her jeep, then retraced back to the side door. *Shelby's nurse didn't call today.*

Maia slid her back against the sun-warmed bricks and waited. *I feel closer to Shelby here than in the car.*

Dr. Ed took the elevator to the ground floor. He hugged his jacket over his white lab coat. He adjusted his mask.

Maia saw him coming. She met him on the sidewalk, masked, with chest out, her neck stiff. "I learned what you and Mom did about the twins."

"We were young."

"You were young?" Maia turned her nose upward. "How young?"

"We were in our twenties." Ed raised his hand in protest. "Look, we did the best we could."

"The best you could, huh?"

Ed swallowed slowly. "The best, we thought."

"The best you could do was follow the advice of the medical experts and your church friends?" Maia sniffed. Her hands framed her hips. "Then why didn't you let me die of my leukemia?"

"Because we loved you."

"And you didn't love them? Because my first two sisters didn't fit your plan?" she accused. "Because I don't? Because Shelby doesn't?" Her rant turned sarcastic. "Because Dana wants to transition?"

Ed stretched out his hand toward Maia. His shoulders hunched for a hug. "Look. We did the best we knew, the best we could."

"Well, it wasn't good enough!" Maia backed away, her hand on the bricks on the other side of the door. "Really bad for them too."

Tears moistened his eyes. Ed stretched out his arm a second time. "Maia, can you somehow forgive me?"

Maia turned to face Ed, tore off her mask, and threw it onto the gravel. "To hell with all of you. To hell with this virus. Loving yourselves and using others." She stomped toward the Jeep, her footsteps echoing in the near-empty parking lot.

An early June wind slammed the Jeep door. Maia revved the motor.

I learned in my pre-law class that somebody needs to pay. And payback is sweet.

She grabbed the shimmy of the steering wheel, screeching the wheels as she exited the parking lot. *Vengeance may be God's to repay, but it's mine to deliver!*

***

Ed's eyes trailed Maia's Jeep disappearing among the early summer leaves. He wiped his eyes beneath his glasses. "May God have mercy on us all."

He blew his nose and adjusted his mask, then reached for the door to the hospital.

Dr. Ed Clarke pushed his glasses atop the mask, up the bridge of his nose. The door latched behind him.

A tunnel of spattered windows arched over the empty hallway.

His second home. Maybe his actual home. Where sick people supposedly come to get better. But caregivers get worse and lose everything.

The grate of Ed's shoes softened from the tile to the carpet.

There has to be a better way.

62

Shelby heard a rustling outside her door. Sounded like something soft being put on. She opened her eyes to the dim ceiling, to what little she could see in the dark. Tiny flashing lights of red and yellow reflected in the cabinet across from her bed. She heard occasional beeps from a machine above her head.

There is this enormous tube in my throat. It's still hard to breathe. But that sledgehammer to my ribs has stopped. She thought to feel her toes. Something felt like it moved the blanket near the bottom of her bed. Her hands couldn't move very far. *There are straps around my wrists.* But her right thumb felt something like a button. She pushed it.

More bustling. The door creaked open. Heavy breathing. A large presence halted by her bed.

"Well, it's about time that sedation wore off," a tired voice said. The presence wore a badge that said Nurse. *Is my waking up a joy or a chore?*

"I'll call the respiratory therapist to evaluate your breathing."

So began days of weaning evaluations and explained medication adjustments—all meaningless to Shelby.

The nurse arranged phone times with Greg and the kids. A sister named Maia called repeatedly.

Therapy meant pushing through tears to get the body to work again. *Things you never think about—automatic things. Now very hard.* To get the lungs to work, the arms to steady your hands to your mouth, the legs to hold your weight. *Most of all, something, please, anything—to get my head to stop hurting, my ears to stop ringing.*

Humiliating. *Feels like I'm two or three years old again.*

Days when I can concentrate are almost worse. I can't get my body to do what I tell it.

Pain, just to make the body move again. Weariness. Pounding against despair. *Better to be alone when I cry. It would be worse if Greg and the kids knew how decrepit and old I've become in just three weeks.*

The bed scale weighed twenty pounds down. Shelby looked away and blinked her tears. She swallowed. *Being fat is better than being weak.*

* * *

Greg didn't want Shelby to go to a rehabilitation unit. He wanted her home. He made a list of all household and other chores Shelby had done. He called a family meeting. Each person took six items, six responsibilities they would do for five months while Shelby recovered.

No exceptions, no excuses.

The kids, even at ages eight and nine, thrived with these jobs. They finished online classes in record time, competing to find online treatments, pretending they were therapists. Their mom wasn't the most agreeable patient. Maybe somebody in the family knows something about psychology?

63

"What the hell you doin' with all that stuff? I thought when you left with that guy, you was outta here for good." Auntie Rosalynn marched into the bedroom, cigarette dangling, to the ashtray on top of Tanya's boxes in the corner. "You was off to that college. Gittin' a little too big, I'd say."

"I was at Mom's for the last six weeks." Tanya steadied her shaky hands. She looked up to face her aunt. "And now, I'm here."

Auntie Rosalynn inhaled the last of the cigarette and damped the stub into the ashtray. "The last time you came here was when your daddy got shot and your momma couldn't pay the rent. That's what happens when you take a high-paying job with the police department and move to where you don't belong."

"Last time was a little different." Tanya steadied herself, four fingers on the dresser's ledge.

"It's a good thing I still live here and let you stay. I keep a good place, you know."

A July breeze billowed the sheer curtains through the window. In the front yard, weeds bordered the chain link fence. The bouncing of a basketball, on the court outside, drowned the playground yells and the heavy bass of a boombox.

"Then you all had to move in with me. In the projects. Had to go to our school," Auntie Rosalyn snorted. "So much for your preppy school. No uniforms here."

Auntie Rosalynn parted the sallow lace curtains and rolled up the blind. She drew three bottles of rum from under the bed and stashed them between her armpits and her generous bosom. "Need a little help for my fruit juices. Warmer weather lately."

Auntie Rosalyn turned to leave. "You can pull down that blind when it gets dark. A little more privacy if the bangers are busy tonight."

Tanya lay on the bed, studied the cracks across the ceiling. *The pipes likely busted sometime past.*

She bumped into the trash can on her way to the bathroom. *Will this spotting never stop? It's been seven weeks since the procedures.* She held out her arm in the scanty light and fingered the implant—well healed.

A dog barked in the neighbor's yard. Tanya heard Auntie Rosalynn answer the door. Fake laughing, glass bottles clinking. Auntie padding toward the kitchen.

Tanya fumbled to the mirror, filled the sink glass with tap water, and guzzled it. *Something has to change.*

She walked to the bedroom corner, removed Auntie Rosalynn's ashtray, and opened the first box. A brown stuffed animal, a puppy, greeted her from the top. She held it to her chest and closed her eyes. *My sixth birthday party. Candles and balloons. A cake with my name on it.*

Tanya pulled out the puppy and perched him on the dresser. She sniffled, tears streaming down her face and dripping off her chin. *Lots of hugs. I can still smell the sweat on the collar of his uniform.*

She tore the lid from the second box in fury. She dumped the contents on the bed beside her. *A very different sweat from Jethro as he jammed himself inside me.*

Makeup and false eyelashes deep in the bottom. *Clothes too big from my last shopping spree. Shoes too wide—no longer fit. A different time.*

Box three. *College clothes from fall 2019. My clothes. Finally.*

Tanya scooped up the makeup and eyelashes and headed for the cabinet next to the sink. Yelling from the street. A muffling of gunfire.

Things have to change.

The mirror reflected pale lips and baggy eyes. "Oh, God—maybe that God of my grandmother's church—any god will do, as long as I get out of here."

She grabbed the television remote control from the bed stand. The first flash—an advertisement—showed buff young people parachuting from airplanes, getting college degrees, being saluted.

"God or no god, that was a fast answer!"

She collapsed to sleep on the bed. Without taking down the covers.

64

Representative Wm. J. Jackson had scheduled a call. *At the rehab? With Jakeem? Whatever for?* He couldn't get into the facility because of the virus. But he left a message with the activities director that he would like to visit Jakeem online.

William Jackson came on the screen and told the director he'd already had the COVID. Done survived it. Wasn't afraid no more.

The webcam showed both men with the beginnings of wrinkles and hairlines turning gray. They reintroduced themselves.

Jakeem scratched his memory head.

William Jackson had grown up three floors down in the Projects. In the hood.

He done good. Maybe too good. Didn't fit in the hood no mo. Not that he ever has to go there.

Can't even go there without creatin' a situation. Can't ride the bus in his fancy suit, can't wear his nice shoes, can't talk right anymore. Even the bus driver knows he don't belong there no mo.

Jakeem dug deeper in his memory head.

William Jefferson Jackson did good in school. He always talked about his daddy giving him a whooping if he didn't do good or got into it with the teacher person. At least he had a daddy.

He did basketball, got a scholarship to State, and went to law school. Then into politics. Jakeem hadn't seen him in years.

Jackson was a talker. *That hadn't changed.* Jakeem was still short of breath. He nodded, his eyes bobbing to the floor.

Entertaining and powerful speakin' in the hood—must have helped William Jackson with his lawyering.

"Yeah, I be shifting the ladder."

"Shiftin' the ladder?" Jakeem's eyes came to the camera.

"Well, I be on a ladder to a high window. Gotta keep climbing."

"Yeah, I'm on a different ladder." Jakeem shifted in his wheelchair. "To a different window. I'd just like to see my kid and have my woman."

"Well, you can have lots of women on the ladder I'm on." *Wm. Jackson always knew how to brag.*

"Yeah, well, I can still speak like I want and ride the bus to see what I want."

"There is something to be said about that," Wm. Jackson wrinkled his forehead. "Part of leavin' behind anything is no longer fitting in—no longer fitting in where you are going or where you came from. Kind of lonely."

"Like the prophets from my momma's Sunday class. They be lonely folk."

"Yeah, lonely. They say it's racism, but the same thing seems to happen to the Asians and Latinx. Even the Whites. When they leave the perch they're born on, they have a lonely life. No place to return. Never fit in where they been or where they're going. It's good for their kids, though."

The camera showed William Jackson stretching, adjusting his suit jacket, repositioning his tie, fumbling with his mask.

"Well, I thought I should let you know about the new funding for job retraining. It'll be more school, but you can use your hands, not your back, to earn your place at the table."

"Sounds good."

"It won't change your ladder entirely, but you will reach a different window."

"And if I fall off?"

"The hood be soft to land you."

Jakeem thought of his woman, his daughter. *Maybe a different ladder, a different window. Maybe he could rescue his child from the hood after all. Yes, it would be lonely. You could get more money if you blamed it on race or the economy or bad luck—being born at the wrong time in the wrong place.*

The truth be—all adventures are lonely. You never return, from even an online adventure, with the same eyes that saw the world before. You always have different eyes. Maybe that's a good thing, even if it be lonely.

William Jackson said his office could fax the forms on Monday. A nurse walked by. "There's a fax machine with a printer in the staff office," she offered. She looked at her watch.

Time for the visit to end. *Rules. Rules made by white supremacy?*

If Jakeem could get his COVID brain fog to clear, the world—with or without forms or any ladders—would be a lot easier.

* * *

Jakeem had weeks of rehabilitation. *I used to work in a place like this. Now I'm a patient.* He tried to remember stuff, but his brain fogged; his head still hurt. Every day. His ears sounded like crickets having a party. *Not invited to their party.*

Despite many tests and exhausting efforts, Jakeem couldn't care for himself. *Let alone care for others.* He couldn't stand long enough to help distribute medications. And he didn't have the strength to catch a falling resident. With every attempt to exercise, to get stronger, he felt worse. *Just the opposite of the high school gym.*

His career as a CNA was over. So much for climbing the ranks of the profession. Couldn't remember enough for more schooling toward his old goal of RN.

Jakeem spent mornings in therapy and afternoons in the anteroom—watching the fishbowl, staring blankly into the water.

A Pastor Jim happened by, to wave through windows at his parishioners, to bump elbows, or to pray with those comfortable seeing a human from outside the facility. Pastor Jim waved himself beyond security, spouting that his last negative test for the virus was this morning. But he wore his mask and gloves. And he had the cosmic suit with him, in case some frightened person wanted him to put it on.

Pastor Jim spotted Jakeem beside the fish tank.

"How are ya, bro?" asked the big-bellied man. His skin was chocolate, his frizzy hair escaping his man-bun. He had on a full sleeve shirt despite the July heat. *Gang tats. Likely need to cover these for some of the places he's going today.*

"Makin' it." Jakeem forced an answer. "Barely."

"Discouraging, isn't it?" ventured the pastor.

"Yeh, like being a fish, swimming in unknown waters, never leaving the cage." Jakeem stared ahead. "And I used to consider myself a people person."

"Well, the governor says there's a break in the restrictions," the parson offered. "We're having food this Saturday. On the house."

Jakeem stared at the floor.

Pastor Jim continued, undeterred. "Might be good to see some people other than those here and eat some different food too."

"Sounds like a change." Jakeem looked up for the first time. "Got a wheelchair van? Pick me up?"

"Got the van. Got the people to help get you inside. Seven-thirty?"

"Deal."

Elbow bump.

* * *

Five a.m. came early on Saturday. But Jakeem was ready. His nurse was ready too. She had Jakeem dressed, his shoes on, his adult diaper hidden under street pants with belt and polished buckle. *She must have a cheerleading outfit underneath that nurse's uniform.* She adjusted his mask as the van came.

The ride wasn't the smoothest and the city looked strange. Jakeem hadn't seen it in weeks. He didn't remember it this way.

"Are you sure you know where we're going?" he asked the driver. The streets were still mostly empty, occasional cars sneaking around, acting as if they were afraid to be there, but owning the place, all at the same time.

"Oh, yeah, I know where we're headed." The driver rounded a corner and stopped.

The pastor with the gang tattoos and the long-sleeved shirt greeted the van. Jakeem found himself inside with lots of good-smelling foods.

But the assortment of folks was odd, and masks made it harder to sort them out.

There were Asians speaking some sing-song language. Black folk from Africa mixing up Swahili and French. Lots of Spanish. There were some older kids running around speaking their own languages. Some hefty white lady said these kids made up their own languages in the refugee camps. She said you should try French if you really needed to say something to them.

Jakeem rubbed his head. "I don't remember much from French class."

There were ladies in hijabs, with masks overtop, shouting at their kids in what sounded like Arabic. That white lady said this was hardly a halal meal, and she knew they couldn't have any pork or gelatin. But they were welcome to eat whatever they could.

Jakeem had already found the mouth beneath his mask and finished two plates of bacon.

"More bacon for me." Jakeem smiled at Pastor Jim.

People were still eating, kids running everywhere. Guitars started at the front, with lots of reverb from the mikes. A couple of American black ladies with smooth singing started swaying to some tune he had never heard before.

Jakeem started swaying in his wheelchair. His left foot actually grooved with the music.

The minister with the long sleeves that covered his tats took the microphone. He said a prayer, thanking God for the food and for a place to meet, that many had their jobs back. Some had the rent postponed, so they didn't have to move, and they still had family around. Some people got sad on the part where he remembered all those who had died. But people were reminded to be thankful that the new strain of the virus was milder and that the government had promised a vaccine by Christmas.

Then, a man, a whitey, had the guts to pray for forgiveness for all the bad things Whites had done and ignored that hurt their brothers and sisters. Next, a big black dude, who'd obviously done time and done some people—given his eye and cheek tattoos—took the microphone and asked God to forgive all the black folk for preaching hate and benefiting from baiting others with their color. Some folks clapped. For both.

Jakeem had never heard such prayers. *Ain't nobody clapping for praying like that. Especially in Momma's church.* Jakeem shook his head and adjusted the knob on his wheelchair.

And the governor just said white people needed to do the heavy lifting. Jakeem adjusted his mask.

Some Asian dude read from the Holy Bible in his own sing-song language, then in some brand of Chinese. Some really black man from Africa read the same passage in Swahili. Some Middle Eastern type read the passage in French, then Arabic.

The minister with the long sleeves spoke next. "We should care for each other, pray for each other, and be the hands and feet of Jesus to each other. This pandemic will pass, but the Good Lord said His Word will never pass away. We need to learn what the Good Lord is talking about."

Some white guy, who hardly looked like a bouncer, managed the door. He came to where Jakeem was sitting.

"Say, dude, you have a computer?" the white guy asked.

"Yep."

"Well, you have good fingers and a mending brain. We could use some help to route the food deliveries to those shut in from the virus. Would you like to help?" He smiled. "The pay is nothing, but the happy molecules are better than white powder."

"Sounds good. When can I start?"

"What about Wednesday? The food comes in on Tuesday night. One guy here owns a local grocery. They give us any leftovers, but we need to get it out before the weekend."

Jakeem headed to the entrance and the van.

He noticed a very white chick with blue hair run into the place. Her eyes looked lost. A pink mask hid her face.

"Hey, you," he yelled at her. "Who you lookin' for?"

"Tanya. A friend named Tanya. I took the bus, thinking she might be here."

"Ain't seen her," Jakeem grinned. "But I'll keep looking."

65

Laura brought the kids home as soon as COVID restrictions were relaxed—on Ben's next weekend off-call—as planned.

She was happy. Or at least she was laughing.

"Hey, partner," she teased. "Brought home some steaks. The grill needs some workout too."

She washed the salad, her breasts to the sink. Ben liked her butt. He missed her. He really did.

Ben retreated to the pantry and took several deep breaths.

He scanned the deck. His three kids chased each other down the hill, pretending their water pistols were laser tags. *Such a visual. Worth over three cruises on the French Riviera.*

The family had a quiet, candle-lit supper. The kids were hyper from the cramped car ride. They needed to blow off steam. An uphill walk proved the ticket.

The breeze was still cool. The mosquitoes weren't warm enough to swarm, the gnats too cold to congregate. Ben looked at the setting sun, suddenly happy. He had one day off. One day to cherish all this goodness before heading back to the swamps of dying and dread. He took a deep breath and wished away the transient flash of ventilators and dyspneic patients pleading for air. This air was his, for this moment.

The walk ended. The kids took quick showers and made it to the loft before they collapsed.

Ben studied Laura in the semidarkness. It was her night. He needed her to tell him about Florida. She didn't need to hear about New York for the past four months. A new viral strain would replace the one that had died with the patients. Laura didn't need to know about the refrigerator trucks still parked behind the hospital.

She had married Ben, not the hospital, not medicine.

He took her hand, and she started to talk. The night became morning before she fell asleep, mid-sentence. Ben covered her gently with a shawl her mother had made.

Dr. Ben Lawson stared at his hands. How many patients had these hands intubated? How many had these hands saved? Worse, how many had died because he intubated them, thinking he understood this virus? Before even expert doctors understood this virus?

And how many died because he wasn't in charge at all? After all?

He paused. To watch Laura's breathing, to memorize her eyelashes with her eyelids closed. He needed to remember her cheeks, her nose, how her hairline met her brow.

I will never take Laura's breathing for granted. Ever again.

Ben turned off the lamp.

He rolled onto his back to face the ceiling. *How can I be so lucky as to have such a beautiful woman? A beautiful woman who will still bring my kids home to me after such an abyss has been crossed?*

66

Out of this city. Subway to the bus. Homeless people. Jobless people. Hopeless people. Heading to a better place? *At least a place with cheaper rent.*

Maia dozed.

Until the bus suddenly jolted.

Maia grabbed the metal sidebar. The door opened.

A disheveled man with a soiled backpack and two shopping bags stumbled onto the bus, landing in an aisle seat, a stale odor following him.

The man ranted through his lopsided mask. "We are all unfinished characters, thrust mid-drama into unknown scenes with no script. The only script we have is in our heads, our own adaptability." He paused, his mask wobbling with his headshake. "I would just like a different costume, a different stage."

Impressive words for a homeless bum. Homeless artist? Drama professor down on his luck?

The man suddenly stood.

"You think you're going to do better than the family you came from," he grumbled as he shoveled his bags toward the landing.

Maia watched him.

He zigzagged his gaunt frame toward the side door, then steadied himself before he fumbled down the steps. He turned around to grab his backpack and bags from the first step. The bus door closed and the bus lurched forward. The back window showed him sorting his bags briefly on the sidewalk, then heading into some bushes. His stench hung in her nose.

The bus turned again, still heading out of the city. Maia caught the driver's eye as he checked the rearview mirror.

The bus lurched at the corner five blocks down and pulled to the curb. A woman in military fatigues boarded. A younger man with a little girl also boarded.

Maia shifted her gaze to the handrail above her head. *Is that man on the same trajectory as my family?*

She lifted her chin. *I can make a better family.* She sat up firmly in her seat. *Perhaps with Jonathan.*

Her eyes traveled to the woman in military fatigues riding alone on the side bench. Starched, freshly ironed military fatigues—buff, muscular, no makeup, no fake eyelashes, her curly hair in a ponytail. She arranged her military pack on the empty seat beside her. The brown fur of a stuffed toy escaped the zipper in the upper pouch. A familiar last name tagged above the left breast of her uniform.

"Hi, stranger," Maia hesitated. "Where have you been? I haven't seen you in a while."

Tanya's eyes hurried to the driver's mirror. "I just finished basic training. On to my first assignment."

"That's great!" Maia regrouped. "I'm glad you're better."

"Yep, one way to get Uncle Sam to pay my tuition."

"Good idea!" Maia nodded.

"Yeah. It's one way to be armed." Tanya headed for the midsection door. "And legal."

Tanya got off the bus at the next stop.

Maia's eyes dropped to a ratty stuffed puppy wobbling near the midsection stair.

67

I am sinister, a pretender. Devious, even demonic.

I am the spiny creature in the closet lurking to find you when you least suspect me. Hiding, I disrupt systems, spew cytokines, and make clots where none should be. I kill doctors, patients, and dreams.

I am rearranging the futures of all creatures, not just those I infect.

I am unpredictable. They easily manipulated my image for political and career gains. I preclude the laws of nature and of medicine.

Just look at what I have accomplished in such a short time.

College campuses are empty, save for lurking killers and muggers, while students struggle to see beyond the blue lights in their bedrooms. Doctors struggle with inadequate supplies, logistical jams, and never-dreamed-of plans. Even when they have supplies, I defy the laws of predictability and baffle science.

Science is too slow to study me, and statistics are too obtuse to tell people what they really want to know. I will mutate and transform my image before they can capture me. I am the ultimate sleuth.

My greatest weapon is fear of me. Just think, cancel culture infects the entire world, including the world of medical thinkers, humans who are so self-assured they limit options, study obtuse ideas, and miss my weapons.

Well, they don't really limit my options. I will prove them fools with weapons they can't see because they close their minds, and thinking themselves wise, they prove to be fools. They think their brains, awash in chemicals which they minimally construe with their diets, beverages, sex, and sleep—they think their brains will figure me out. But they are created creatures, just as I am a created creature. But my base has been here longer than they, and they are naive.

I am the mongoose who has outwitted the cobra.

But I can also be the cobra, kept in the kitchen to kill the rats, only to have my poison kill the people too, when I strike. They have thought that bats and caves and pangolins nurture me. But where I came from and where I am going, they can't figure out. There is nothing new under the sun.

They have forgotten the old. I am a master at camouflaging the old and masquerading as the new. They have sequenced my proteins and copied my backbone, but they have never figured out the gloves I use to reach where I don't belong. Thus, I can wreak havoc in machines from human bodies to economies to societies.

I am the fear of death, old but disguised as new. I cause hysteria and chaos—not only because of what I can truly do but because of fear of me.

Their evolution limits humans to be less than their options. They are living with residua of their brains, deluding themselves that they are improving, but denying realities that exist beyond puny measurements.

I will take this spiny form, as it serves me currently. The greatest brains of the time will attach their significance, their reasons to be included in the protected community of humanity, to their knowledge of me. The experts will attach these to me.

But in time, I will become a household word, a limited eponym flagging this time of discovery. Their children will not care about their contributions to this history.

Then I will take another form, designed to trigger humans into their own conceit and waste their limited lifespans on machines. A simple electromagnetic pulse or loss of electrical current can render such machines obsolete.

Their heroes amuse me. They do not know how childish is their pursuit and how trivial their lives. If they only knew. But with their canceling of any thoughts not allowed by the elites among them, they will never know.

They will blunder in the dark, always afraid of the spiny creature in the closet, not sleeping because of the imaginations in their heads.

I smirk.

68

The new society. The new normal. A society of "likes." And "dislikes." Emoji thumbs up, emoji thumbs down.

A new fear. Fear of being canceled by unknown trolls prowling social media. Virtue signaling, depending upon which virtue they extolled today. The old soup du jour.

The new way to God or to be a god. God or You is what you decide him or her or it to be. One path? No. Outdated. Totally intolerant. Not inclusive.

"Bullies," Shelby would call them. *I can hear her now.*

"Children in adult bodies, playing games with the fragile selves of others. All anonymously, using created or real names, to avoid being punched back."

The new playground—since we can't go to a real playground anymore. After all, schools are still closed.

Our minds may never reopen.

69

"I hoped I could reach you before you get too far out there," Shelby panted. "I'm not asking where you're going. I just know you need a cell tower if we're going to chat."

"I can still hear you." Maia adjusted her earbuds.

"I just made it back to the wheelchair," Shelby puffed. "This oxygen tubing is quite the tether, but I stood for six minutes at the kitchen sink."

"So you made it out of the wheelchair today?" Maia quizzed.

"Yep, another milestone. Doesn't sound like much to most people," Shelby chuckled. "But look, I've survived COVID, gotten off dialysis, gotten off the ventilator. Gotten home—thanks to my hubby and my kids."

"Yeah, that's pretty amazing."

"Someday, I'm going to dance before the Lord. As the Psalmist says."

Maia twisted her lips and glanced in the rearview mirror. *You've got to be kidding! Shelby spiritualizes everything.*

"Say," Shelby's voice sounded stronger, less winded. "I wanted to thank you for hanging those yellow curtains at the kitchen window. The gray ones were getting pretty drab."

"No big deal. You ordered them. They were delivered. I just hung them."

A robotic voice interrupted from Maia's phone. "Turn right at the next exit."

"Oh, wow! Bees just darted in between the flowers near the window," Shelby prattled. "I'm so grateful you planted them close."

"No problem."

The line buzzed. Message on the dash screen: "No signal."

Must have gone around a mountain.

70

The wind battered the bent sign ahead. Its message peered through the dust. Another right turn.

No signal, huh? Out here in the middle of nowhere.

The warning light for the fuel gauge pinged yellow a second time. *Different car. Not the Jeep. Likely real.*

Maia glimpsed the sleeping Jonathan, contorted in the front seat. Then the baby camera clipped to the rim of the rearview mirror. Chloe made her licking sounds from the middle seat.

The dust vortexed a clearing. On the left, a one-stop shop with two fuel pumps. Maia veered, her tires hitting gravel.

Chloe continued licking her paws, settled on her pad in the second seat, pillows wedged against the chaos of the back.

The mountains glowed sunset pink through the windshield ahead.

Maia stopped, unbelted, and jumped out.

The fuel nozzle at the one-stop shop was rusty. But it worked.

A gush of fuel pulsated through the line, guzzling into her tank. She looked down at an estimated three inches of dust clinging to the chipped concrete of the pump's foundation. She tapped her toes.

Fumes of the gasoline drafted upward. *Wretched place.*

A grizzled old farmer drove his rusted-out truck into the bay on the other side of the pump station. *That truck must have been red in its day.*

He climbed out, then blew his nose on a ragged hankie from the pocket of his grease-stained overalls.

He rattled the hose of the pump on his side.

Gasoline now chortled from both hoses. *Distracting sound. Like elevator Muzak.*

Maia looked toward the highway, nose lifted. *Maybe some fresh air?*

The old man lifted his hose as if to drain the last ounce of petrol, then replaced his nozzle. He eyed Jonathan stuffed in the front seat, then at the empty fingers of Maia's left hand as they held the nozzle.

He studied Maia and winked. "There's a wedding chapel some twenty miles up the road, on the right."

The old man kicked each tire, then slapped the truck's fender. "Faithful. Yep!"

A dust twirly danced around the rear of the truck, but the caked dust continued to cling to the numbers on the rear plate.

The passenger-side door of the truck screeched open. The old man's head bobbed as he stooped, the sound of empty cans shuffling from the floor space. He rounded the front to the driver's side, then patted a fender again. This time gently.

The old man hefted his obese frame into the driver's seat, box springs sneaking through the tattered upholstery to snag the leg of his overalls. He freed it with an index finger jutting through the frayed edge of his glove.

He started his truck. It backfired.

No muffler.

More fumes.

Maia looked south, steadying her fuel nozzle against the wind.

The old man and his truck whined out of the gas station. They billowed southwest, a tunnel of dust trailing after them.

The gas pump was now unprotected from the wind. Brown grit blasted into Maia's hair. Clouds rolled near the rim, threatening a rain squall.

Maia slammed the nozzle into its stanchion, then stuffed cash into the dusty envelope shoved in a side window. She crammed into the driver's seat.

The spatter of rain left flecks of dirt on the windshield. *Not gonna clean the windshield here.* No snacks from those machines, either. *Not from this place.*

She turned south. *No signal. No radio.*

She adjusted the cruise control. *I wonder if there is an old-fashioned atlas, or at least a paper map, in the glove compartment?*

The mountains turned purple, the foothills gray.

Tracks from the old man's truck still lingered in the dust on the road.

"Marriage, huh?" She smirked. "Sounds like more commitment than pleasure."

Jonathan snored in the front seat.

"Right now, there's very little of either."

Chloe continued her licking sounds from the middle seat.

Maia glanced at Jonathan the second time. *A good man—makes a living, doesn't drink or smoke too much, doesn't do drugs, doesn't womanize.*

No cars ahead. No cars seen in the rearview mirror. *Maybe not so hot, but he tries to be a decent provider.*

The last glimmers of the sunset timbered over the mountain. Lights speckled the valley. *Jonathan is like a comfortable shoe. Good for a long walk.*

A wooden snow fence hunkered against the August wind on the ridge. A tumbleweed raced across the road. The car swayed to the left, then back to her lane.

The passengers continued to sleep.

Hope. Maybe. After all.

Another flurry of rain. Drops of water, scalloped by dust, clouded the windshield.

Maia fumbled for the wipers and steadied her foot on the accelerator.

GLOSSARY

Anesthesiologist: A physician with special training to keep the body safe and the psyche unaffected during a surgical procedure

APACHE II score: An estimate of ICU mortality based on certain laboratory values and patients' signs accounting for both acute and chronic disease manifestation

Bicarb level: a marker for acid-base status in the body

Bougie: a thin cylinder that a physician inserts into or through a body passage; in this case, the airway for endotracheal intubation

BMW: The acronym BMW stands for Bayerische Motoren Werke GmbH, here used as the name of a luxury car.

CBD: abbreviation for cannabidiol, a component of the marijuana plant, noted for its help in the management of pain and certain types of seizures

CRISPR: a tool for editing genomes, allowing alteration of DNA sequences and modification of certain gene functions

CRRT: Continuous renal replacement therapy. Used to support failing kidneys when the blood pressure is too low, or the patient is otherwise unstable; for renal dialysis in a designated unit

Conjunctivae: The membranes over the white of the eye

CMO: Chief Medical Officer. Usually a physician-administrator in charge of managing a hospital regarding medical decisions

COVID: Severe acute respiratory syndrome coronavirus 2, shortened to SARS-CoV-2. COVID became the WHO designation for the virus as of 2/11/2020.

CO2 Monitor: In critical care, End Tidal CO_2 monitoring is used to assess adequacy of circulation to the lungs.

CNA: Certified Nursing Assistant

CT scan: A diagnostic imaging scan that uses a combination of x-rays and a computer to create images to look inside the body

EHR: Electronic Health Record

ER: Emergency Room

HIPAA: The Health Insurance Portability and Accountability Act of 1996 (HIPAA) is a federal law that requires the creation of national standards to protect sensitive patient health information from being disclosed without the patient's consent or knowledge.

Intensivist: A physician with subspecialty training in internal medicine, often pulmonary medicine [study of lungs] or spending almost exclusive time and training in the intensive care unit

ICU: Intensive Care Unit. A block of rooms designated for unstable and sick patients needing frequent physician visits and bedside procedures, including mechanical ventilation and bedside dialysis

IV: Intravenous, through the vein

Laminar air flow room: A room for infectious patients where the air is contained to limit infections to others

M.D.: Medical doctor

MRSA: Methicillin-resistant staph aureus. A bacterial infection that can become airborne, ultimately related to staph

N-95 mask: A facepiece respirator mask filtering 95% of airborne particles that have a mass median aerodynamic diameter of 0.3 micrometers. Initially used in industry and requiring fit testing for the individual. If used in situations of infections, it is to be discarded after one use.

Nasogastric tube: a tube inserted through the nose to the stomach

OR: Operating Room where surgeries performed

PhD: Doctor of Philosophy

PPE: Personal Protective Equipment. Usually a gown, mask, gloves, sometimes a face protector, designed to minimize viral exposure during the pandemic of 2020

Quentin: A large catheter through which high volumes of blood or dialysis can be undertaken. Placed in patients where kidney therapy or rapid infusion of blood products may be needed

Reflex mallet: A rubber triangular tip with a metal handle, used for detecting changes in neurologic reflexes

Suboxone—narcotic substitute used for maintenance or tapering therapy for individuals suffering from substance use disorder

STAT: Abbreviation for statim, which means "immediately" in medical jargon

t-piece: A long circular tubing that allows the patient to remain on a ventilator without receiving prescribed breaths. It can be used with or without oxygen or pressures. Often used in attempting to wean a patient from dependency upon a ventilator machine

TB: Tuberculosis, an airborne bacterial infection

Twill tape: Cotton tape used to secure medical appliances